"Love costs too much," Laird said roughly

Anna looked away from him, her face hot, then cold as ice. "Did I ask you to love me? Do you think you're the only one afraid of getting hurt?" she muttered, fighting down the pain she felt.

Laird looked taken aback. "That's just it. I don't want to hurt you," he replied, now flushed and impatient. "To be honest with you, Anna," he whispered as he moved toward her, "I want you so badly— You've been driving me crazy for weeks!"

Anna knew he was offering her passion and sensuality, but not love. He might satisfy her craving for physical pleasure, but it would never be enough. It wouldn't mean a thing if Laird couldn't—or wouldn't—love her.

CHARLOTTE LAMB began to write "because it was one job I could do without having to leave the children." Now writing is her profession. She has had more than forty Harlequin novels published since 1978. "I love to write," she explains, "and it comes very easily to me." She and her family live in a beautiful old home on the Isle of Man, between England and Ireland. Charlotte spends eight hours a day working at her typewriter—and enjoys every minute of it.

Books by Charlotte Lamb

A VIOLATION
SECRETS

HARLEQUIN PRESENTS

HARLEQUIN ROMANCE

CHARLOTTE LAMB

whirlwind

Harlequin Books

TORONTO • NEW YORK • LONDON
AMSTERDAM • PARIS • SYDNEY • HAMBURG
STOCKHOLM • ATHENS • TOKYO • MILAN

Harlequin Presents first edition March 1988
ISBN 0-373-11059-6

Original hardcover edition published in 1987
by Mills & Boon Limited

CHAPTER ONE

ANNA was late for rehearsal and had to run all the way from the bus stop to the theatre in a London suburb at which the production would be opening in ten days. This was the first time they had been able to rehearse there; until now they had been using a draughty church hall in Islington, a short walk from where she lived. That was really why she was late. Her landlady had caught her as she was going out of the front door.

'The rent's due today, Miss Rendle!' She had a voice like a buzz-saw and a face to match; sharp and edged with a great many teeth.

Anna had turned, forcing a placatory smile. 'I know, I'll pay you tonight—I'll get my money today.' She hoped she would; if she could persuade the cashier to advance her salary which wasn't actually due until Friday.

'You know the rules! I can't bend them for anyone. You pay or you go.' Mrs Gawton made the same speech to everyone; it had a ritual ring to it.

'I promise I'll pay you tonight,' Anna said desperately, fleeing before she could be pulled back. She had missed the bus she meant to catch and the next one was late and got caught in a traffic jam. It crawled all the way across London while she sat on the edge of the seat in an ecstasy of anxiety, chewing her fingers to help herself forget she was hungry, staring out of the window at shops full of things she couldn't afford and mentally running through her lines again.

Joey Ross flew into a blinding rage with anyone who was late, with one notable exception, and that wasn't Anna.

When she finally got off the bus she ran full tilt down the narrow, shabby street, still murmuring her lines, her lips moving, her bright red hair streaming behind her, completely unaware of passers-by staring. Some looked twice because she was, apparently, talking to herself in an excited way. Some did a double-take because Anna Rendle was a strikingly beautiful girl: tall, with a supple, swaying body, her features finely modelled and her green eyes enormous. Anna herself wasn't so much unconscious of her own looks as indifferent to them, and to their impact on men. All her drive went into a burning ambition which left no room for other emotions.

Reaching the eighteenth-century theatre whose shabby glitter had a tawdriness in daylight, she dived for the stage door and ran straight into someone coming out. Anna reeled sideways and fell over, hitting the pavement with such a thud that for a minute she just lay there, dazed.

'Are you OK?' a man's deep voice asked, and she opened her eyes to find him kneeling beside her. As Anna looked at him his cool grey eyes wandered from the tumbled mass of her red-gold hair to her pale face and down over the sensuous curves of her body. Anna was accustomed to men staring at her and had acquired an armour against such interest, but she was amazed to find herself flushing under this gaze.

In self-defence she struggled up, pushing away his hands as he tried to help her. 'I'm fine, thanks,' she said curtly, then realised that she had somehow lost

one of her shoes. She glanced around and the stranger
followed her eyes, his brows lifting, fine black wings
above his heavy-lidded eyes. He saw her shoe first and
bent to pick it up. Anna held out a peremptory hand,
but he didn't hand her the shoe, he turned it over
between his long fingers, staring at it, and Anna's
colour deepened again, this time with embarrassment, because the shoe was so obviously cheap and
shoddy. The sole had worn through and Anna had
lined the inside of the shoe with stiff cardboard until
she could afford new ones. She hated knowing that
this stranger could see all that.

'Can I have my shoe, please?' she asked in an icy
voice meant to freeze any comment he might be about
to make.

He shot her one brief look, his lashes descending
at once to cloak whatever he was thinking, then went
down on one knee and held the shoe out. Anna stared
in shock at the top of his sleek black head, unable now
to see his face. Biting her lip, she lifted her stockinged
foot and felt him slide the shoe over it.

He stood up and she muttered, 'Thank you. Excuse
me, I'm late.'

'If you're hurrying to get to rehearsal, it will be
starting half an hour late anyway,' he said. 'Dame
Florence has only just arrived.'

How did he know that? Anna wondered, looking
into the grey eyes and recognising that they had a
formidable authority. Was he connected with the
theatre? She had never seen him before, he didn't look
like an actor, but whatever he was it obviously paid
well, because she saw now that he was expensively
dressed. His wide-lapelled black overcoat had a
smooth silkiness which made her suspect it could be

cashmere; the suit she glimpsed under it was of a
similar quality. He was tall and lithe, but he wasn't
good-looking, far from it; his face had a pared angu-
larity which was forceful rather than handsome; her
eyes assessed that hard mouth, determined jawline,
strong cheekbones, then flicked up to the cold grey
eyes, to find them watching her with irony.

'What do you think?' he asked drily.

'You're not an actor,' she said, admitting that she
had been trying to guess why he was visiting the
theatre.

'No.'

'A director?'

He smiled, a crooked amusement in the twist of his
mouth. 'Not that either. Give up?'

'You're with management?' What else could
explain the wealthy gloss of his appearance? As he
lifted a hand to rake back his thick black hair she saw
a stylish gold watch on his wrist, and caught sight of
the time with a pang of alarm. 'Oh, no, I must go,'
she said, and fled into the theatre without another
word.

She found the cast sitting in a semi-circle on hard
wooden chairs; some chatting idly, others feverishly
reading their words.

To her enormous relief the director was nowhere
in sight—presumably he was attending on Dame
Florence?

'There you are! I thought you weren't going to get
here!' said Patti, her pale blue eyes smiling as Anna
sank on to the chair next to her.

'My bus was late,' Anna explained, taking off her
coat and huddling inside her thick fisherman's
sweater. 'It's cold in here, isn't it?'

'Freezing,' agreed Patti without much concern. She was a very pretty girl with short curly dark hair and a triangular face; her blue eyes large and thickly lashed, her mouth small and pink. Her part in the play was tiny and required little real acting, but she was enjoying every minute of her first stage role and she and Anna had already become friends during the past four weeks of rehearsal. They shared the same obsession; that bond required no other cement. They hadn't yet got around to talking about anything but the play; Anna knew nothing of Patti's private life, nor had she confided to Patti any details of her own. They talked theatre in the breaks for coffee and lunch; shop talk was the only subject interesting either of them at the moment.

'If I get any colder, my teeth will drop out,' Anna said, and everyone laughed.

From the back of the row of chairs a high voice declared piercingly: 'I'm wearing two pairs of long johns under my trousers!'

Everyone turned, grinning, as Dame Florence King swept down towards them; seventy-two years old and as spry as a cricket in her sweater and thick woollen trousers, clutching her script to her flat chest along with a capacious purple handbag, the young director following in her wake like a very small sheepdog with one enormous sheep to cherish. Joey Ross was only just twenty-nine but had already acquired a legend and a reputation for being a brilliantly original director, yet he handled Dame Flossie with kid gloves because in spite of her cheerful camaraderie she could unexpectedly turn steely and cut him down to size if he went too far. She was, after all, one of the starriest stars in the theatre firmament, and for all her professionalism and willingness to listen to his suggestions she never quite forgot that, while Joey knew that Dame Flossie had forgotten more about acting than he had yet learnt and that her instincts were sometimes wiser than all his own clever reasoning.

On this reciprocal basis they worked well together and the company sensed a possible triumph ahead of them all, but the opening night was just ten days away now and the atmosphere was becoming more tense every day.

Smiling at Anna, Flossie advised benevolently, 'Woolly vests help too, dear. They never heat the theatre during the day; it costs too much.' She dropped her script on the chair and her bag on the floor and sat down in the centre chair, left vacant for her by common consent. 'And thick woolly socks and fur-lined boots,' she added.

'OK, everyone,' said Joey, directing his eyes to Anna as if she had been doing the talking, not Dame Flossie. 'Cut the chat now and let's get started. Act Two, Scene Two, if you're all ready. I think you have the first line, Dame Flossie?'

'I think I do, dear boy,' she boomed, immediately at her most professional. 'Unfortunately . . . ' She looked down at her bag, helplessly stared around her. 'I seem to have mislaid my script.'

'You're sitting on it, Dame Florence,' Anna said shyly, still over-awed by the star she had never dreamt she would work with.

Dame Florence leapt up, discovered her script and asked in amazement, 'How did it get there?' Her audience chuckled, she settled down again, giving the director a humble look. 'I'm so sorry, ready now . . . ' She turned the pages with much fluttering and searching, gave Act Two, Scene Two a brief glance and then lowered the script, her enormous, deep-sunk black eyes on the director as she launched into her words without faltering or looking back at the page. She was, of course, word-perfect, although the speech was quite a long one, but the director drily made no comment on this wicked display of one-upmanship. He was well aware of Dame Flossie's predilection for game-playing and dutifully acted as her stooge when occasion demanded; if it kept her interested he would stand on his head and bark like a dog.

The play was a new one and the author had had to rewrite most of the scenes over the weeks of rehearsal. Anna's script was covered with scribbles where words had been changed. Although her part was rather more central to the play than Patti's she only appeared in three scenes and had far less to learn than Dame Flossie; she was deeply impressed by the older woman's ability to memorise her lines and rarely forget a word or gesture or inflexion. Dame Flossie seemed so vague and cheerful, her performance apparently effortless; you got mere glimpses of the work she had put into what she did.

Today's cheese sandwiches were supplemented by a home-made date cake provided by Dame Flossie. 'Now, you don't have to eat it, I cooked it myself, so I can't say it's good, can I?' she chuckled, offering Anna the plate. Anna had made herself eat the sandwich slowly; her hunger was so extreme she was afraid to let it show. She took a slice of cake, murmuring, 'Thank you, it looks delicious,' and nibbled politely. The cake was ambrosial to her; she watched others taking tiny pieces and wondered if there would be any left.

'You must have had a long bus ride to get here from Islington,' commented Patti, having refused the cake with a polite excuse about being on a diet. 'You live in a flat, don't you?'

Anna thought ironically of the square little room which was her only home; shabby secondhand furniture, grimy lace curtains at the windows, a gas ring in one corner, a sink in another, just enough room to swing a cat.

'Yes,' she said flatly.

'Do you share?'

With spiders and woodlice and the odd visiting mouse, thought Anna, but said, 'No, I live alone.'

Patti gave her a curious look. 'Where do your parents live?'

'I haven't got any. They died when I was twelve—a car crash.' Anna opened her script, signalling the end of discussion, and Patti lapsed into silence until rehearsals began again. It was the first time she had ever shown an interest in Anna's life outside the theatre. Anna didn't object to her questions, it was just that there was nothing to say. She had no family, no friends in London. After her parents' death she had lived with foster-parents who had been kind and yet neutral, perhaps because they had been looking after other people's children for years and had learnt to protect themselves by not getting too involved, not giving too much or laying themselves open to pain when the child was taken away again. Anna had been well fed, neatly dressed and sensibly treated.

As soon as she was sixteen she had left and got herself a job in London working in a shop, living in a hostel. She had saved every penny she could and at eighteen had been given a place in a drama school. She had got a scholarship grant, but it had been barely enough to cover the fees. She had worked part-time in the evenings to earn money for food and rent, and at weekends she had worked all day in a hotel as a chambermaid.

Three years of that had stripped her body of every spare ounce of flesh, fined down her features, given her green eyes the burning glow of frenetic discipline. She had been terrified that at the end of her school course she wouldn't get a job in the theatre, but to her amazement she had been offered one at once. It was not what she had dreamt of, but it had paid quite well. She had spent last summer in a seaside repertory company, doing a dozen small parts. At the end of the season she had gone into rehearsal for panto; playing a dancing mushroom in *Puss in Boots,* whirling around the stage in a glittering sequined leotard, carrying a red and white spotted umbrella open over her head, among a crowd of other fairy mushrooms, while the production's comic star tried to catch one of them. Clad in a black cat skin and wickedly flicking his tail, he chased them around, while the audience roared. It was one of the hits of the panto and it had, ironically, got Anna this part in Dame Flossie's new play.

Jocy Ross had seen her and on the strength of that performance had decided she had a flair for comedy and would be perfect for the role of a young girl in his coming production.

Anna's part was not as simple as it appeared on the surface; Joey kept reminding her that it walked a razor's edge between farce and tragedy, so that one step too far either way would be disastrous.

'This is an ambivalent moment,' he said today, stopping her with a peremptory gesture. 'Funny, yes—but hauntingly poignant, too. I know it's hard to get all that in such a short speech, but try it again, will you, Anna?'

She took a careful breath, her body poised while she thought about what he'd said, then she spoke her lines again, and this time Joey didn't interrupt, just smiled, nodding, as the cue was picked up by Dame Flossie.

It was almost seven o'clock by the time rehearsals broke up for the day. Anna and Patti left the theatre together, talking about the last scene they had rehearsed. Anna wasn't on stage in it, but Patti was, and unhappily admitted that she felt hopeless about playing with Dame Flossie.

'I feel like a tiny little candle shining next to a light-house,' she complained. 'She's marvellous and very kind, but when we're alone on that stage, who's going to notice me?'

Anna gave her an incredulous look. 'But you couldn't outshine her anyway, so why try? The play's the thing—on stage you won't be thinking about yourself, you'll be that girl with her grandmother who's slowly dying. That's all you'll have on your mind.'

Patti had stopped listening, though. Her eyes were fixed on something ahead, her face delicately flushing.

Anna followed the direction of her gaze and frowned, seeing a blue and silver Rolls Royce parked at the kerb outside the theatre. The driver slid out of it as she watched; it was the man who had knocked her over on her way to rehearsals. Anna tensed, her nerves bristling—what was he doing here?

He strolled lazily towards them, his powerful body making an impact even at a distance.

'Hello,' he said in that deep, cool voice, but as Anna opened her mouth to give him a dismissive reply she suddenly realised that he wasn't even looking at her, he was staring at Patti, his mouth twisting in an amused smile.

'Oh . . . hallo . . . ' stammered Patti, and Anna watched her pink face with a frown. Patti's mouth was quivering and her eyes were wide with obvious anxiety.

'I was driving this way and I thought you might like a lift,' he drawled with a hint of mockery.

Patti looked down, biting her lip. 'Well, I . . . that was kind of you, but . . . Mr . . . ?'

My God! She doesn't even know his name, thought Anna. Did he pick her up the way he did me this morning? Patti's nervous reaction to seeing him made it clear that she hadn't invited his pursuit but didn't quite know how to get the message over. She was barely twenty, after all, and hadn't had much experience with men, Anna suspected, certainly not with men of this type. The mocking sophistication of his smile had obviously thrown her completely.

'Laird,' he said softly. 'Laird Montgomery.'

Anna laughed; she couldn't suppress it. The name immediately struck her as comical, unreal; she suspected he had just invented it. No doubt he didn't want Patti to know his real name. He was probably married. He must be in his mid-thirties and he didn't look like a confirmed bachelor, more like a husband looking for some action on the side.

He turned his eyes on her for the first time then, their gaze hard. 'Can we share the joke?'

'I was just wondering what your real name was,' Anna retorted blandly.

Patti took a sharp, indrawn breath, giving her a startled look. Hadn't it occurred to her that he might have made up the name? She really was too innocent to be let out on her own; she was looking like a startled fawn now, her body quivering as if she wanted to run away; and that would be by far the wisest thing for her to do.

'What a suspicious mind you have!' he drawled, mouth crooked. 'Talking of names, do you have one?'

Anna's silent smile was derisive. She looked at Patti. 'We'll miss the bus if we don't hurry, are you coming?' Speak now or forever hold your peace, she thought, her green eyes commanding the other girl. Tell him to get lost, you idiot!

Patti lifted her eyes to the man's hard-boned face, slid them towards the luxurious interior of the blue and silver Rolls. Anna could see the struggle raging in her mind. It was a bitterly cold evening; Patti was dead tired—the temptation must be enormous.

She couldn't guess what Patti would decide to do, and certainly didn't expect her to say huskily, 'Could you . . . give us both a lift?'

His face was impassive as he said, 'Of course,' turning to open the rear door of the limousine.

Patti gave Anna an uncertain look. 'OK, Anna?'

'Why not?' Anna was amused by the compromise between Patti's common sense and her desire to have a drive in the Rolls. It was understandable, though; the car was a thing of beauty and it wasn't every day that you got the chance to ride in one.

Patti slid along the seat and Anna got in beside her, the back of her neck prickling as she felt Laird Montgomery watching the way her long legs moved. He closed the door and walked round to get behind the wheel, and Anna glanced at the girl next to her.

'I hope you know what you're doing,' she murmured quietly. 'He's a bit out of your league, isn't he?'

Patti made a muffled sound, bending her head. Anna saw the back of her neck turn carnation-pink, and her mouth indented. The girl simply had no idea how to deal with a guy of his kind, did she?

'Tell him you've got a date,' she hissed. 'Invent something; any excuse will do.'

He had opened the driver's door and was getting into the car. He turned, his arm along the back of his seat, raising one of those fine, winged black brows. 'Where will it be?' he asked Anna, making it very clear that he intended to drop her first and get Patti alone.

Anna looked sideways at the other girl, her eyes enquiring. Patti swallowed, her face lifted and her eyes meeting Laird Montgomery's briefly.

'Could you drop me first? I've got a date tonight.'

Anna saw the flash of surprise in his hard face, the frown and narrowing eyes.

'A date? What are you talking about?'

Patti moistened her lips, very flushed. 'I'm meeting someone in Wolfstone Square, at the hotel.'

'Wolfstone Square,' he repeated drily. 'I see—the hotel, you said? Right.'

The engine purred into life and Anna leaned back, luxuriating in the scent of expensive leather, the deep upholstery, the smoothness of chrome and polished wood under her hand.

'How did the rehearsal go today?' asked Laird Montgomery over his shoulder.

'We survived,' Anna told him, aware that Patti was staring out of the car window in a fixed way as if trying to pretend she wasn't really here at all. Anna had seen birds do that when a cat was on the prowl, freezing and trying to become invisible, only the nervous glitter of their eyes betraying them. She stared at the back of Laird's head angrily. He was a ruthless, selfish bastard, and for two pins she would tell him so. Couldn't he see Patti was too young to cope with someone like him? Or was that the real attraction? Did he get a perverse kick out of making her shake like a leaf whenever he smiled at her?

The car was heading west, the streets much more elegant now, wider and better lit. Why on earth had Patti asked him to take her to this neck of the woods? Had the name just popped into her head? Anna wondered. Patti was in a state of panic, that no doubt explained it. She hadn't been thinking too clearly.

The car slowed and turned into Wolfstone Square to draw up outside a palatial white facade. Anna stared curiously at the portico, expecting to see a uniformed doorman spring down the steps to open the door of the Rolls for Patti, but there was no sign of anyone. Patti clambered past her, saying hurriedly, 'Goodnight, Anna, see you tomorrow.' The door opened, blowing Anna's red-gold hair into a wild tangle. By the time she had brushed it down the door had closed again and the Rolls was swishing round the gardens in the centre of the quiet square. Anna turned to look back, but there was no sign of Patti on the pavement; she must have entered the hotel at a run.

'What's your address, Anna?' asked Laird Montgomery, and she looked back at him, their eyes meeting in the mirror over his head.

She gave him the address tersely and as he turned the limousine northward again she debated whether or not to say something to him about Patti. Was there any point? He wasn't likely to take any notice of her views. She frowned, staring out of the window. On the other hand, Patti was much too nice to get mixed up with a man like this.

She leaned forward and he shot her a quick look, then glanced back at the busy road.

'She's just a kid, you know, why don't you leave her alone?' Anna said bluntly. 'She doesn't know the score yet, she's as green as grass—why not leave her that way?'

She saw his wide shoulders stiffen under that cashmere overcoat and his hands tighten on the wheel as the car slowed at traffic lights on red.

Turning, he asked harshly, 'What on earth are you talking about?'

She laughed with deliberate disbelief. 'You don't know? Come off it, we both know what you were after! She's half your age, you know, and quite out of your league.'

His eyes glittered. 'But you're not?' Anna froze as his stare ran insolently over her. 'Are you offering me an alternative entertainment for the evening?'

'No, I am not!' she broke out, her face burning.

'No?' His derisive smile got under her skin; her hands curled into fists.

'No!'

'I was planning a candlelight dinner for two,' he drawled. 'It would be a pity to have to eat alone.'

'That's tough,' Anna said wrathfully, turning to the door. 'You can forget that idea!' As her hand reached out, the traffic lights turned green and the Rolls moved off smoothly, at speed. She sat on the very edge of the seat, her body tense, her brow furrowed. He had just admitted tacitly that he was planning a little seduction tonight. The dinner for two had certainly not been intended to end with the coffee and liqueurs. Patti didn't know how lucky she had been; if Anna hadn't been with her as they came out of the theatre Patti would be sitting here now, no doubt in a state of acute panic. Staring out of the window, she sensed that they had stopped moving into the poorer areas in which she lived and were headed back west again into the exclusive district of Mayfair.

'I am not having dinner with you,' she informed him icily.

He laughed. Anna did not like the way he laughed, either; it sounded too much as if he thought she was just playing a game, pretending to be hard to get.

'I'm serious! Stop this car, I want to get out.'

'I've ordered caviare,' he said conversationally. 'With toast and chopped boiled egg and onion, and lemon, of course.'

'Caviare I can take or leave,' Anna said cuttingly.

'And champagne, of course,' he added.

'The bubbles make me sneeze.'

'And then I thought we'd have a Chateaubriand steak,' he went on as if she hadn't said anything.

Anna suddenly thought of the small tin of baked beans waiting for her at home; she had been debating whether or not to sprinkle a little curry powder into the beans, just to change the flavour a little. They were full of nutrition and immensely cheap, but she ate them so often.

Steak, she thought, her throat moving convulsively as she imagined it. Am I crazy? Here I am starving for a square meal and I can have one if I . . .

The Rolls suddenly spun and began to move down a steep incline into an underground car park.

'Where are you going?' she asked in alarm as he pulled up and parked in the shadowy vault. He didn't answer, merely slid out and slammed his door, came round and opened hers. Anna stayed glued to her seat, her eyes dilated and her body shivering, all her bravado gone. She wasn't afraid of Laird Montgomery—she was scared of herself. Tempted by all that lovely food, she didn't know if she could handle this.

'Do you want a formal invitation?' he asked mockingly. 'Very well.' He bowed, offering one well-shaped hand. 'May I have the pleasure of your company at dinner?'

'And afterwards?' Anna muttered feverishly, trying to calculate her chances of fighting him off later.

'I'll drive you home.'

The cool reply made her stare uncertainly; he met her gaze without blinking, his mouth wry.

'If that's what you want,' he added, somewhat spoiling the effect.

'It *will* be what I want!' Anna threw at him with vehemence, and knew that she had made her decision and that Laird Montgomery was aware of it too. He was smiling with bland satisfaction; but if he thought she might change her mind once he had poured some wine into her he was going to find he was mistaken. Anna might have dinner with him, but that was as far as it went.

CHAPTER TWO

THE lift shot upwards at a rate that made Anna gasp, her stomach still on the ground floor. 'What is this place?' she asked, and Laird Montgomery's reply made her stiffen.

'An office block.'

'A what?' asked Anna in a rising voice.

'A large block of offices. We're going to the top.' His smile was teasing. 'Isn't that where you're aiming? The stars?'

Her suspicions were aroused again; she didn't trust this man. 'What's at the top of the building?' She had imagined that they were going to have dinner in some swish restaurant, for some reason coming to the conclusion that the underground car park belonged to a big London hotel and that when she emerged from the lift she would find herself in an elegant, *crowded* foyer. If this was instead a block of offices she had an appalled suspicion that there were not going to be any comforting crowds around wherever they were headed; she was going to find herself alone with him.

'We're going to have dinner in a penthouse flat,' he drawled, and Anna leapt for the button panel.

'Oh, no, we're not!'

Before her finger hit a button, he had caught hold of her wrists and was tethering them at her sides, smiling down into her flushed, agitated face with mocking enjoyment.

'No need to get hysterical. You're not about to get raped.'

'I don't intend to be!' she spat out, writhing in his grip and finding it impossible to break out

'What sort of monster do you think I am?'

'I've no idea—what sort of monster *are* you?' she muttered, avoiding the gleam of the grey eyes. He still wasn't good-looking, but she had a nervous feeling that she found him attractive, and that wasn't good. 'I don't even know who you are,' she wailed. 'I don't believe that that's your real name; it can't be. Nobody could have a name like that. It's a stage name.' Then her eyes flew to his face, startled. 'Are you an actor, after all?'

'I have never set foot on a stage in my life,' he said as the lift doors slid open and he hustled her out, her feet dragging as if she were a reluctant child being taken to the dentist.

Her eyes flashed around the corridor into which they had emerged: smoothly carpeted, well lit, silent. Worrying.

'Who lives here?' she demanded, and got the answer she had dreaded.

'Me.'

'Just you?'

He smiled, one hand still circling her wrist and pulling her along like a slave girl going to the auction block. 'Just me.'

'Take me back to the car!' Anna snapped angrily, trying to run back to the lift. He refused to relinquish that grasp of her and leaned over to press a bell beside the only door in sight. Nothing happened. He put his finger on the bell and kept it there, frowning.

Anna began to calm down, watching his scowl with relief. He wouldn't be ringing the bell if he had a key, and if he didn't have a key they couldn't get in.

'Let's go and have a hamburger somewhere,' she suggested in a friendlier voice. 'Pity about the Chateaubriand, but I'll be perfectly happy with a hamburger.'

He wasn't looking so charming now; the teasing little smile had vanished and he was as black as thunder. 'What the hell is going on?' he muttered, banging his fist on the door. 'Parsons!' The roar made Anna jump and watch him anxiously. He wasn't going to turn violent, was he? And who on earth was Parsons?

'Open this damn door, Parsons!' Laird yelled, and as he did so, the door did open and a very small, stooped old man peered out at them as he shrugged into a white jacket.

'What's all this then? No need to bellow. I was coming.'

Laird had let go of Anna and was advancing angrily on the old man, snarling at him. 'You've been at the bottle again!'

'I 'ave not.'

'I can smell it, damn you! Can't I trust you an inch? Do I have to send you to that drying-out place again?'

The old man did up his white jacket and straightened his few white strands of hair with a supercilious sniff. He was just tall enough to come up to Laird Montgomery's top shirt button. His face was a yellow waxy colour, his nose bulbous and his watery eyes flecked with red. He was not a pretty sight, even when he began to do a fair imitation of a butler.

'Good evening, sir, good evening, madam,' he intoned, staring straight ahead at nothing. 'May I take your wrap, madam?'

Very tempted to giggle, Anna began unbuttoning her coat and Laird automatically moved behind her to slide it off her shoulders. Tossing it to the old man, he said curtly, 'We're having dinner.'

'Yes, sir,' Parsons said, dropping Anna's coat and slowly bending to pick it up. Anna almost expected to hear him creak, but he managed it and straightened again, holding her coat. She flushed slightly as she saw him peer at it incredulously; it was as old and shabby as her shoes.

'Caviare,' snapped Laird. 'With all the trimmings.'

Parsons scratched his chin. 'I think I got a jar in the fridge, but I'll have to boil the eggs.'

Laird ignored that. 'And then a Chateaubriand.'

'A what? I 'aven't got a bit of steak in the place!' Parsons protested indignantly. 'I wasn't expecting you, was I? If you don't let me know you're dropping in how am I supposed to have Chateaubriand handy? Think I'm a mind-reader or something?'

Anna looked hard at Laird, whose angular profile was all she could see; that still betrayed a faint flush. He had been lying about the candlelight supper for two, or else he had brought her to a different place? She felt her nerves prickle—was that it? Had he brought her here with something other than dinner for two in mind? The building below them was silent and dark; everyone had gone home, leaving the offices empty. Up here on this penthouse floor they were as isolated as if they were on a desert island, and

Anna began to feel flutters of panic in the pit of her stomach.

'What *have* you got?' Laird asked through his teeth.

'I'll 'ave to look and see. I got a freezer full of stuff. Trout or veal or . . . look, leave it to me and I'll rustle something up.' The old man shuffled along the polished woodblock floor of the hall in which they had been standing. He threw open a door and Laird walked towards it with Anna's hand held tightly in case she ran away.

'It seems a pity to put that poor old man to so much trouble,' Anna said as Parsons closed the door on them. 'Why don't we go out and have dinner somewhere?' Somewhere busy and full of people, preferably.

'I don't pay him to get drunk every night, it will do him good to have work to do.' Laird stalked over to a black and gold enamelled cabinet and threw it open. 'What would you like to drink?'

She stared at the array of bottles uneasily. 'Nothing, thanks.'

Pretending not to have heard, he reeled off a list of drinks. 'Manhattan? Gin and orange?' he ended, and Anna shook her head. She hadn't eaten anything except one cheese sandwich and a slice of cake in the last twenty-four hours and she knew that any alcohol she drank would go straight to her head. In fact the very idea of food made her feel faint, and as Laird swung frowningly to glare at her she heard an embarrassing rumble from her stomach, and turned bright pink, walking away in the hope that he might not have heard it too.

The room was rectangular and high-ceilinged, very spacious; one wall all window, the lace curtains drawn over the glass but a dazzling view of London's illuminated skyline visible from up here. Anna walked over the deep-piled white carpet and stood at the window, staring out.

She heard Laird walk out of the room, the door closed quietly, and she spun round, startled. Where was he going?

Being alone gave her a chance to stare openly at the furnishing and décor; it was expensive and modern but had no particular character. She was faintly disappointed; she would have expected him to have a more distinct taste in style. Black leather couch, deep-upholstered chairs to match; a low glass-topped coffee table—it had no personality whatever.

The only interesting object in the room was a bookcase on the wall opposite the window. Anna slowly wandered over there, studied the titles curiously—an odd mixture of novels, biographies and poetry. She pulled out a collection of sixteenth-century verse and the book fell open of its own accord at one page, as though it had often been opened there. Anna's eyes caught the first lines of a poem and a smile of surprise curved her lips.

'They flee from me that sometime did me seek . . . '

Was Laird Montgomery a Wyatt fan? Anna closed her eyes, her low voice huskily murmuring the words, their melancholy echoing in her mind. She knew it by heart; it had been one of her audition pieces long ago.

She didn't hear the door open or the man who entered the room walk slowly towards her, listening intently.

The first she knew of his presence was a smell—a delicious, tormenting smell which Anna for a few seconds imagined to be the product of her fevered imagination. Her nose quivered and she sighed, then jumped several feet in the air as Laird Montgomery spoke at her elbow on the last syllable of the poem.

'Eat this while it's hot.'

Her eyes dropped to the plate he held out. On it lay a perfect semi-circle; golden and fragrant with herbs and cheese. It was the most beautiful omelette she had ever seen and it wasn't the mirage she had believed it to be. She put out a finger and touched it; it was hot.

Laird Montgomery walked over to the coffee table and put the plate down, offering her a fork. Very flushed, she walked to join him, biting her lip, furious with embarrassment because he had realised how hungry she was, but dying to taste the omelette all the same. Hunger had little pride, she thought grimly, and sat down without looking at him.

'Thank you,' she muttered, head bent.

'You spoke the Wyatt beautifully,' he merely replied, and walked out of the room again, leaving her to eat in peace.

By the time she had finished every last scrap she was feeling very friendly towards him. It had been tactful of him to go, and as he came back she smiled wryly at him, her head back against the black leather couch and her body relaxed and warm and fed.

'That was delicious! Parsons is a terrific cook, I haven't enjoyed a meal more for years.'

He was carrying a tray on which stood a glass of milk. He put that down, glancing drily at the empty plate.

'How many meals have you had lately.?'

She coloured but laughed. 'I'm on a diet,' she lied. 'Perhaps I went a little too far.'

They grey eyes watched her sardonically. 'Drink your milk,' was all he said, however, then he strolled over the to enamelled cabinet and picked up a glass of whisky, walking across the room again with it and sitting down next to her on the low couch. Anna had already swallowed half the milk; contentment invaded her and she became aware of the physical and mental weariness which hunger had kept at bay for hours. She had been working so hard during the last month; permanently at full stretch and using up every last ounce of energy during rehearsals, but not replacing it with enough food because she couldn't afford to spend a penny on anything but the bare essentials. She had learnt during her years in London to eat the cheapest foods: porridge for breakfast, baked beans for lunch and supper, an apple here, some milk there. Going without meals had become a habit; she had to pay the rent and her fares. Eating was dispensable.

'Do you live alone?' Laird Montgomery asked her, sipping his whisky, and she turned her head sleepily to nod.

'In a flat?'

'One room,' she admitted frankly. 'A bedsit. It isn't Buckingham Palace, but it's home.' She laughed, her nose wrinkling at the memory of it, but Laird didn't smile.

'Where do your family live?'

'I haven't got one.' She linked her hands behind her head, her chin tilted and the full rich flood of her red-gold hair spread over the black leather cushion.

'I'm a little orphan,' she said lightly, mocking herself.

'Nobody at all? Not even one relative?' he asked, his brows lifting in that winged fashion which made his face so memorable.

'None that I know of . . . ' She told him about her parents and he listened, his face shuttered and unreadable, betraying none of the pity Anna would have found so unbearable. She hadn't told anyone about her background before, except in curt explanations when she was asked a direct question, because she hated people to feel sorry for her. It irked her pride, and that dislike of pity was one reason for her burning ambition—if she became a star, nobody need ever feel sorry for her again.

That wasn't the only reason, of course; her drive to the top answered all her problems. When she made it and saw her name in lights, she would be safe, she would never be hungry or worried about paying the rent, she needn't wear cheap, shoddy clothes or be cold and lonely in a bleak little room.

She had very different reasons for choosing the theatre as her route to security—subconsciously aware that she could have picked another way, gone into business or become a model. Quite apart from wanting to be rich, Anna was passionate about acting. It fulfilled some need she felt; gave her a chance to escape from herself, gave her an enthralling mystery to unravel, the secrets of another human being to glimpse. She loved language, delighted in expressing it with her voice the way she had murmured the Wyatt poem a short time ago. The theatre gave her far more than just a hope of reaching final security; she knew she would have become an actress even if she hadn't needed success. It had always been what she wanted, right from the first play she ever saw.

'What did you do before you got this part?' Laird asked, and she turned her head to smile at him lazily.

'I was a fairy mushroom.'

His brows flicked up. 'What did Parsons put in that milk?' He leaned forward and picked up her empty glass, sniffing suspiciously at it.

Anna laughed. 'I'm serious—I really did play a fairy mushroom in a panto. It was rather fun, actually, and the pay was good. I ate well while I was with them.'

He leaned back, his head turned towards her and his arm along the back of the couch, his long body casually relaxed beside her so that their knees touched. He wasn't smiling, though, his eyes were cool and thoughtful.

'How much do you earn a week?'

Normally she would have prickled at that question and refused to answer, but she was in a soporific trance conjured up by warmth and good food on top of bone-cracking weariness, so she told him cheerfully, and he frowned.

'And your rent? What's that?'

Anna as calmly replied and was surprised when he swore. She stared blankly at him then. 'Why are you so angry? Try and find anywhere cheaper, mister! That is the bottom of the market, let me tell you, I'm lucky to have got it.' She made a little face. 'And today's rent day and I haven't got the money, so when I go to work tomorrow my landlady's going to be lying in wait for me and I shall have to think fast and talk fast to stop her chucking me out.' She didn't sound too worried. Ever since she moved in there she had had the same running battle with Mrs Gawton; she always paid her rent within a day or two and she felt sure the woman would give her the usual time to find the money. Seeing the dark frown on Laird's face, she went on lightly, 'Don't worry, I'll get the money. I've asked for an advance on my salary and they'll give it to me, they always do in the end.'

'It sounds to me as if you permanently live ahead of your income,' Laird said grimly.

'Who doesn't?' Anna looked sideways at him, her mouth curling. 'Present company excepted, of course. You obviously don't have to live hand-to-mouth, lucky you; some of us aren't so fortunate.' Her green eyes mocked him. 'Maybe it was time you learnt how the other half lives—I'm broadening your education.'

'Thank you,' he drawled, watching her with narrowed eyes. 'Let me do the same for you.'

Anna had forgotten her suspicion and doubt of him over the last hour, her worries lulled by the food and the way they had talked. She wasn't prepared for his swoop, she just stared helplessly at his face as it came down towards her, her eyes focusing on his hard mouth.

As it touched her own she stiffened in shock, as if she had touched a bare wire and had had a massive jolt of electricity sent through her veins. His arms closed round her, pulling her down with him as he sank backwards on the couch, his mouth moving coaxingly on her lips, parting them, the kiss a heated intimacy against which Anna found she had no defences.

She didn't even know she had shut her eyes at first; she thought that the velvety darkness into which she fell was one consequence of that kiss. She was shaking violently, her hands clinging to his shoulders and her ears singing with a strange music. It didn't occur to her that it was the sound of her blood running far too fast, but she found the wild responses of her body to his lovemaking increasingly disturbing.

It was the first time a man had ever kissed her, except as a stage exercise. Whenever anyone had tried in the past she had firmly repelled them, never tempted to experiment with any of the men she had met. The married ones she froze with a few biting words; the others more gently but just as decisively. Anna had no room for love in her scheme for living; perhaps if she had tried the occasional fling she might not have been so completely dazed by what Laird was doing to her.

Her inexperienced mouth trembled as his lips finally released it, but Laird didn't move away. He raised his head and stared down at her, and Anna opened her eyes to look at him in confusion, very flushed. She found she was seeing very hazily; his hard-boned face just above her seemed much further away, veiled in mist, yet even so she glimpsed the arrogant satisfaction in his eyes and the curl of his mouth, and a wave of rage swept to her head.

'Don't think . . . ' she began, and Laird put a hand over her mouth, stifling the words.

'Neither of us is going to do any thinking,' he promised ominously, and before she had a chance to bite him she felt his mouth moving along the side of her throat and the pleasure she felt drowned all her protests. His hands slid under her sweater and she moaned as they cupped her breasts silkily, the warmth of his flesh burning into her own. Her stupid eyes had closed again, her body quiescent as he caressed it.

'Put her down, your supper's ready,' grated Parsons from the door, and Anna turned dark red in embarrassment as Laird sat up, one hand impatiently pushing back his ruffled black hair.

'Don't you ever knock before you come into rooms?'

'I did. You was too busy to hear me,' Parsons retorted. 'Now come and eat that caviare while the toast's hot.'

'I should have left you in the gutter where I found you,' Laird muttered, getting off the couch.

'That's nice, after I've spent an hour slaving away over a hot stove,' grunted Parsons, stumping out of the room.

Laird looked down at Anna who was straightening her clothes with shaky hands, her eyes averted.

'There's no need to look like that,' he said flatly. 'Parsons is very discreet.'

She slid off the couch, hot-cheeked and icily angry with herself, with him. 'I'm sure he is—he'd need to be if you're always bringing your women up here! Can I have my coat, please? I'm leaving right now.'

'You're going to taste a little caviare, first,' Laird said, taking her arm in an unbreakable lock, and she struggled uselessly as he pushed her across the room to the door.

'I've already eaten, thanks! I couldn't eat anything else.' Anna was scared; she had told Patti that she would be out of her league with Laird Montgomery, but it was as true for her. While he was kissing her just now she had realised that she was way out of her depth. Her senses still hadn't recovered from his

onslaught on them; she had to get away from him
before he had an equally disastrous effect on her feelings. He was the first man she had ever felt might do
that; she had never had to guard her heart before, it
hadn't been in any danger. Now she knew it very well
might be—and she wanted to run as fast and as far
as she could to get away from him.

He pushed her into the hallway and into another
room on the far side, effortlessly controlling her in
spite of her angry attempts to free herself.

'Parsons would never forgive you,' he informed her
drily, pushing her down on a chair at the polished
walnut dining-table.

It was laid for two, there were red candles burning
on it, their soft light glimmering on silver cutlery and
crystal glasses. A bowl of white roses made a centre-
piece; Anna stared at them incredulously,
remembering the wintry weather outside in the
London streets. She put a trembling hand out and
touched the smooth, cool petals; one broke off and
fell slowly on to the wood, reflected in the gleaming
patina.

'Just have a spoonful of this,' said Laird. 'Do you
like caviare?'

'I've never tasted it,' Anna confessed honestly,
looking down at the glistening black pearls on the
plate between the small piles of chopped onion and
the yellow and white crumbs of egg. She forked a little
of each into her mouth, savouring the mingled
flavours slowly while Laird watched, amusement in
his eyes.

'Well?'

She swallowed. 'Interesting, I don't know if I like
it—but it's different.'

'Different from what?' he asked, as if very curious about her reactions.

'Baked beans!' Anna's green eyes glittered in the candlelight; mockery dancing in them. It was funny, wasn't it? she silently asked him to agree. His life-style was so many light miles from her own; they came from different planets, but as she went on eating the salty, crunchy caviare she decided to let her senses have full rein just for an hour more. She might never have such an experience again; why push it away untasted? Her eyes wandered around the elegantly furnished dining-room again and she sighed with enjoyment. It wasn't going to be easy to go back to her shabby room after this, but tonight she would sleep with a full stomach.

Parsons appeared and whipped away their plates, substituting clean ones on which he laid wafer-thin veal in a delicate cream and mushroom sauce and some broccoli and puréed carrot.

Laird had poured champagne into a fluted glass beside Anna's plate, and she sipped tentatively, avoiding Parsons' eyes. No doubt he thought she would be sleeping with Laird tonight; how many other girls had he seen at this table, having candlelight dinners for two?

When he had gone she tasted the veal, expecting it to be delicious and finding she was right.

'Did you really find him in a gutter?' she asked, and Laird laughed.

'Quite literally, yes. He was a chef at one of London's best hotels for years, I met him then, but when he started drinking heavily he lost his job and his wife left him for another man, taking their two children with her. Parsons went to pieces, I gather.

He was blind drunk for about two years when I met him again—he fell under my car and lay in the gutter, so stoned he couldn't even speak.'

He refilled her glass and Anna thirstily drank half of the sparkling wine. 'He's a terrific cook. How did you sober him up?'

'Sent him to a place I'd heard of,' he said, finishing his veal and leaning back to watch her. 'Could you manage a dessert, or have you had enough?'

Anna pushed her own plate away, giving him a little smile. 'I haven't eaten this much for years, but . . . what is the dessert?'

'I'm not sure.' He leaned forward and filled her glass again and she shook her head cloudily.

'Oh, no, I've drunk too much champagne already.'

He made no comment, sipping his own with his black lashes down against his hard-boned cheek. She watched him in the candlelight, her senses singing. Why had she thought he wasn't good-looking? She couldn't have been seeing straight. He wasn't the cinema heart-throb type, admittedly, but his face was intensely sexy. It radiated a magnetism she had never noticed in a man before; the clear-cut lines of it kept her eyes busy and her pulses busier. She liked the way his thick hair grew from a distinct widow's peak; his heavy-lidded eyes were mysterious, but it was his mouth she kept looking at again and again, remembering the demanding pressure of it, the heat it had built up inside her as it moved along her neck.

He looked up and she quivered, looking down, picking up her glass and drinking more champagne as if she had a mouth full of ashes.

Parsons returned and Laird asked him, 'Any dessert?'

'Crêpes Suzette suit you?' growled the old man as if insulting him. 'Or isn't that good enough for yer 'ighness tonight?'

Laird looked enquiringly at Anna. 'Would you like some crêpes Suzette?'

She couldn't resist them. 'Yes, please,' she said greedily.

When Parsons had noisily exited, Laird asked her with a crooked smile, 'Another first for you?' and she nodded.

Parsons cooked them at the table; Anna watched, fascinated, as if at a first night. The old man's gnarled hands were amazingly deft as he grated orange and lemon peel into the pan, stirred the sauce, slipped the delicate pancakes into it and added cognac and Grand Marnier, before setting light to it and standing back to let Anna admire the blueish flames for a second. She leaned forward, breathless, then the whole show was over, the flames doused and a triangular pancake sliding on to her warmed plate.

'*Voilà,*' said Parsons.

'Don't show off,' Laird told him, and the old man took his trolley of equipment and sulkily left the room.

At the door he paused to glare back, and Anna said, 'It's the most heavenly thing I've ever eaten, Mr Parsons.'

'I 'ope you 'eard that,' he told Laird with a sniff. 'Some people appreciate my cooking.'

'Leave the bottles,' Laird merely replied.

Parsons came back to put them on the table in morose silence before slamming out.

Laird met Anna's reproachful stare with a grin. 'Argument is the breath of life to him, it reminds him of his wife. If he wasn't wary of me, he'd be back to a bottle of Scotch a day at my expense. As it is, I keep him down to the odd glass stolen when he thinks I'm not watching. He's too old to reform, now.'

'I think you're very mean to him,' Anna said, regretfully eyeing her last mouthful of crêpe. 'How old is he exactly.'

'Seventy this year.' Laird watched her drain her glass, his eyes rueful. 'I think you've had rather too much champagne. A strong black coffee is what you need now. We'll drink it in the sitting-room.' He came round and pulled back her chair as she began to get up. Anna turned her head to shake it at him, laughing.

'There's nothing wrong with me.' She clutched at his shirt as the room spun and Laird's arm went round her. 'Oh!' Anna moaned, shutting her eyes. The floor was heaving up and down as if it was alive and breathing; it was a nauseating sensation. 'I don't feel very well,' she groaned, leaning on him. 'I think I ate too much.'

'Hmm,' she heard him murmur, and after that there was nothing, her body slipping into a warm darkness.

She woke up with another groan, her head thudding as she turned over in bed.

A minute later she was rigid, lying there listening intently to the distinct and terrifying sound of breathing right behind her. Her foot shifted an inch and touched another foot. It was bare. So was hers.

She shut her eyes again quickly, trying to convince herself she was dreaming. She tentatively moved her hand next; explored her hip and felt silky material. It wasn't a dream; she was wide awake in a strange bed wearing just her slip, and there was a man in bed with her. She knew who it was without needing to look, but she had to see with her own eyes before she would admit it could be true. She very slowly turned her head and in the shadowy half-light of a large bedroom she saw Laird Montgomery's dark head buried in the pillow next to her.

CHAPTER THREE

HER heart beating so hard her breast seemed to shake with it, Anna began to slide her legs out of the bed. She didn't want to make any sudden movement which might wake the man sleeping next to her; she had to get away before he woke up, before she had to face those arrogant, mocking eyes and be forced to remember what had happened in this bed last night.

Her clothes lay on a chair by the window. She crept over to them and gathered them up, turning to steal towards the door. Laird Montgomery shifted his position, the regular sleeping breathing altered slightly, then he gave a deep sigh and Anna froze, watching the ruffled black hair with fixed attention. After another minute she felt safe to move again; she tiptoed across the room and opened the door, her teeth clenched with the effort of doing so without making a sound.

She dressed in the hallway, standing near the door in case she had to make a flying exit. Where had the old man put her coat? she wondered desperately, until she saw the cupboard at the end of the hall. She investigated stealthily and with a pang of relief saw her coat hanging in it.

Five minutes later she was in the street and running to an underground station she spotted as she left the car park, getting a puzzled and suspicious stare from the attendant.

It was only as she passed the massive entrance, with its marble pillars and towering glass windows, that she saw the name of the company whose offices were housed in the building.

She stopped in her tracks, white-faced and incredulous. Montgomery & Sons Ltd?

Montgomery and *sons*, she thought, wincing. He was married and had sons? Or was he one of the sons of an older Montgomery? The company name finally clicked home in her mind as she began to run again, putting as much space between herself and the man with whom she had spent the night as she could. She had seen the huge, glossy boards throughout the city every day without taking much notice of the name, nor had it even occurred to her to connect Laird with one of the biggest construction companies in the country.

No wonder he had a penthouse at the top of the headquarters of the firm! Was he the man who ran the company? Or just one of the family who owned most of the shares?

On the train she huddled in a corner, shivering as if she had 'flu, her eyes on her watch. She would just get to the theatre in time for rehearsals if she stopped off to have a cup of coffee somewhere first; a strong black cup of coffee. That might help her headache and the sick feeling in her stomach.

She tried not to think about last night, but images kept flashing through her head, a strange discordant video playing her memories of Laird filling her glass, smiling at her, talking to the old man, kissing her.

Kissing her. She shut her eyes, her throat burning with the shame and rage. She would not think about it. She would push it all out of her head and pretend it had never happened, and it did have a dreamlike shimmer when she remembered the candlelight, the roses, Laird's smiling grey eyes seen through the gentle, flickering flames. If it had ended there she would have had an exquisite dream to take away with her instead of this pain and anger.

There was a workman's café near the theatre, often frequented by the cast, although not usually at this early hour. The woman behind the counter gave her a nod and a friendly greeting.

'What can I do you for, ducks?'

'Coffee, please, Amy. Black and strong.'

'Dear me, morning after the night before? Don't tell me—you theatricals are all the same.' Amy pushed the coffee across to her, grinning. 'Don't I wish I had your luck? That'll be twenty-five pence, darling.'

Her teeth aching with the forced smile she had felt she had to give the other woman, Anna took her coffee to a far corner and sat down with it, brooding as she sipped. It was ironic that she had saved Patti at her own expense. That will teach me to think I can handle *anything*, she told herself bitterly. I couldn't handle Laird Montgomery, could I? I didn't even know where to start. *He* handled *me!*

Her face burned as the words echoed in her head. She got up and went into the little washroom at the back of the café, used the lavatory and then washed and put on some make-up to hide her deathly pallor. Her green eyes had a hectic glitter as they stared back at her. She barely recognised herself, reading the new knowledge in her wan face and hating the man who had educated her last night. 'What sort of monster do you think I am?' he had asked her, and she had been fool enough to laugh and ask: 'What sort of monster are you?'

Well, now she knew, didn't she? He was a ruthless, unscrupulous bastard under his charm and his smiles and his teasing glances, and she had been bewitched by all that until she forgot her wary suspicions of him and walked headlong into his honeyed trap.

She walked out of the wings just as the director was asking where she was and received one of his cold stares when she slipped into her place.

'Have you got a watch, Anna? Well, can you remember in future that it tells the time, and make sure you aren't here at a quarter past ten when I've called the rehearsal for ten?'

'Sorry, Joey,' she said huskily, her head down.

She felt Patti looking sympathetically at her and couldn't meet her eyes. She was terrified of what other people might read in her own face. She felt that last night was indelibly stamped there for everyone to read.

After Joey had given them his usual brief chat, they discussed the scene they would be doing; where they had gone wrong yesterday, what changes they had to make, and then rehearsals began, but Anna found it hard to concentrate. For the first time, her own life intruded into her role, and by the end of the morning Joey was eyeing her with leashed impatience.

He suddenly burst out, 'Nine days, Anna! Nine days, that's all—and then we open. You're simply not giving this scene your whole mind. I know you're tired! We're all tired! *I'm* tired, my God, I'm tired!' He ran his hands through his curly hair, tearing at it. 'But I'll stay here until the crack of doom if necessary.

we'll do it once more, please, Anna, and this time make me feel it. Get into this, girl! Don't just mouth her words like a ventriloquist's dummy.'

Anna swallowed her words, her face very pale, and went through the scene again, but Joey was not satisfied.

'No, no, no!' he shouted half-way through. 'Anna, for God's sake! What's the matter with you? Somebody pinch her for me, make sure she's awake, because she's acting like a sleepwalker!'

Anna couldn't take any more, she burst into tears and ran off stage, taking refuge in one of the tiny, claustrophobic dressing-rooms where people put their coats. She sank down on a stool in front of the dressing-table and put her head on her hands, sobbing. The garish light of the unshaded bulbs around the mirror glittered down on her red hair, tipping each filament with gold.

She was quiet when Patti came to find her and sat down next to her, shyly watching Anna renewing her make-up with hands that had the slightest tremor in them.

'Are you OK?'

'I haven't cut my throat.' Anna ran a comb through her hair and patted it into place. Her brittle tone didn't fool Patti.

'We've broken for lunch. Joey has gone off for an hour to have lunch with the management and the others have voted to have a pub lunch. Coming?'

Anna shook her head. 'No, thanks.' She didn't have enough money but had no intention of saying so.

'Oh, do come, Anna—Dame Flossie is standing us lunch today, it's her birthday, she'll be hurt if you don't come.'

Anna couldn't say no when it was put like that. When she and Patti emerged from the theatre the others were already trooping into the pub across the road, Dame Flossie leading them like the Pied Piper with his flock of dancing children. Even at that distance Anna could hear her sweet piping.

'What did you think of Laird?' asked Patti, making her stiffen. At Anna's sideways glance Patti flushed, adding hurriedly, 'Laird Montgomery, you know, last night?'

'I know who you mean,' Anna said flatly, her own voice taking on colour. Patti's question had reminded her that the other girl had met Laird first. She hesitated, biting her inner lip, then plunged. She had to warn Patti; what had happened to her last night must not happen to Patti too.

'Look, I don't want to be too heavy about this,' she muttered, 'but don't accept any more lifts from him.'

Patti gave her a startled look. 'Why not? What do you mean?'

Anna found it hard to put into words; she didn't want to tell Patti the whole truth, but she couldn't let her walk blindly into Laird Montgomery's lair.

'You're not a kid,' she said. 'Do I have to draw diagrams?'

Patti gave her another quick look. 'Are you warning me off?'

'What do you think I'm doing?' asked Anna, then saw that there was a temporary lull in the flow of traffic, and darted across the road towards the

Victorian public house into which the others had vanished. The previous landlord had mounted a gaudily painted ship's figurehead above the door and added windowboxes full of sad geraniums to the grimy façade, but nothing would make the Old Britannia look anything but what it was—a working man's pub once haunted by sailors in the days when London's river was crowded with ships, but now fallen like the river on hard times.

As they halted outside the swing doors, Anna was amazed to see Patti giggling. 'I never thought you'd ever be jealous of me!' she laughed and Anna went red.

'That wasn't what I meant! Look, I'm trying to warn you about him. The man's only got one thing on his mind, and I don't mean a kiss at the door when he takes you home. He plays adult games, and he means to get what he wants, he plays very rough. Don't accept any more lifts from him.' She paused, frowning at Patti. 'Unless, of course, that's OK with you. At least I've warned you.'

Patti looked as if she had been dipped in boiling oil.

'What did he . . . ' she began, then broke off, biting her lip.

'*How* old are you?' Anna asked her wearily.

Patti took the question at face value. 'Nineteen . . . nearly.'

Even younger than Anna had imagined, and she made a face. 'Well, use your imagination to fill in the gaps. I don't want to give a lecture on the subject, but you're lucky it was me who went on with him last night, not you.'

About to walk into the pub, she stopped, a new idea coming into her head. 'By the way, how did you meet him in the first place?'

'I . . . my father introduced us,' Patti stammered, still obviously very embarrassed. 'Well, not exactly that—but he was with my father when I came along and . . . '

'Your father?' Anna stared at her. 'So it wasn't at the theatre? I got the idea that Laird had something to do with the management.'

Patti looked confused. 'Well, in a way . . . '

'In a way, what?'

'He . . . didn't tell you?'

'Tell me what?' demanded Anna, becoming even more irritated.

'He's one of the backers,' Patti said in a low voice. 'Don't tell anyone, will you?'

'Oh, no!' Anna exclaimed, her face appalled. 'He's backing the play? Our play?' If Laird Montgomery was one of the backers, there was no way she was going to be able to avoid him if she saw him at the theatre—or pretend they had never met! Not only could he walk in and out of the theatre as he chose, it might make her life very difficult if he was hostile to her.

'But you won't tell anyone, will you?' Patti said hurriedly. 'He doesn't want people to know. He has a phobia about getting his name in the newspapers, and he's afraid a gossip column would pick this up, and people would start hanging around the theatre, to pester him.'

'By people you mean journalists?'

'Yes.'

'A debatable point,' Anna said, grimacing.

Patti laughed uncertainly, too keen to get her message home to find that very funny. 'You won't tell anyone, promise, Anna?'

'Not a living soul,' Anna said absently. 'You know, I never have seen his name in a newspaper, now you mention it, and it's unusual enough, heaven knows. In fact, I'd still suspect he invented it if I hadn't seen the name of his company on that building.'

'What building?' asked Patti, looking understandably bewildered.

Anna gave her a dry look. 'The office block where he took me last night—you won't believe this, but he has a penthouse suite on the top of his company headquarters, just the perfect spot for a little candlelit dinner and seduction.'

Patti's lips parted and she stared, blushing. Anna could see she was at last beginning to get the point, so she didn't dwell on it any further. If Patti accepted a lift from him again, she would at least be doing it with her eyes open.

'Well, let's go and find the others,' she said, pushing open the swing doors of the pub, and at once hearing her name chorused by the rest of the cast who were sitting around two tables in a corner.

'There you are! Hurry up, we're ordering—shepherd's pie or curry?'

'Shepherd's pie,' Anna and Patti said in harmony, and the landlord grinned and asked what they'd like to drink before vanishing.

It was only as she was eating the minced beef with its golden crust of mashed potato topped with cheese that Anna wondered how Patti's father knew Laird.

She looked sideways; Patti was watching Dame Flossie, who had launched into one of her hilarious anecdotes about a famous theatre knight from an earlier decade.

'Is your father in the theatre?' Anna asked casually, and Patti's head swung round, she looked startled, then laughed, her eyes dancing.

'Good lord, no! Daddy was a builder.'

'Is that how he met Laird Montgomery?'

Patti nodded. 'Yes, Daddy did some work for Laird's company. If you knew my father, you'd realise how funny it is . . . imagining he could be an actor, I mean! He's only interested in two things —roses and bees. He retired six years ago, he has had a bad heart and his firm got too much for him, so he started growing roses. He wins prizes with them and Mummy say she's sick of honey—the garden's full of hives and although they sell most of the honeycombs Daddy likes to see his own honey on the table.'

One of the cast tapped a knife hilt on the table. 'Quiet, everyone! I want to propose a toast. Dame Flossie, a happy birthday and many, many more of them!'

They all lifted their glasses and echoed the toast, then sang 'Happy Birthday to you . . . ' watched, smilingly, by everyone else in the pub, some of whom joined in with gusto. Dame Flossie was one of the best known, best loved faces in London's theatre, and people wanted to show how they felt about her.

She glowed happily as she rose to make a little speech. 'Thank you, darlings. You're very sweet and I love working with you—every morning I get up feeling old and tired and then I come to work and your enthusiasm and energy makes me young again; you charge up my failing old batteries! With your help I firmly intend to reach my century and get that telelgram from the Queen.'

They clapped noisily and she sat down, flushed and excited—visibly delighting in having a receptive audience.

Ten minutes later they hurried back across the road, dodging cars, with cheerful grins at the irate drivers, and found Joey waiting for them, tapping his foot ominously, a smouldering volcano in his eyes, but Dame Flossie gave him her most enchanting smile and threw her arms around him.

'Now don't be cross, Joey! We've been celebrating my birthday and we're only a few minutes late!'

He eyed her, his face sardonic. 'You're a wicked old woman,' he accused, but shrugged. 'OK, I'll skip the lecture, but can we please get down to work and no more time-wasting?' His gaze moved to Anna. 'Now, Anna, shall we go over your scene again?'

By the time they left the theatre that evening, Anna felt like chewed string. For a second as she walked out into the chilly night she had a sinking suspicion that she would see the blue and silver Rolls pulled up at the kerb, but there was no sign of Laird Montgomery and she caught her usual bus home.

Her landlady was waiting for her, one ear cocked for the sound of Anna's key in the lock. She shot out like a spider when a fly unwarily crashes into its web.

'Miss Rendle!'

Anna was ready for her, and she turned, and smiled triumphantly. 'Oh, yes, the rent, Mrs Gawton.' She opened her handbag and counted out the money into the waiting hand. The cashier had sent for her that afternoon and advanced the sum she requested. She would just have enough left to pay her fares and buy a little food until Friday.

Mrs Gawton clutched the notes with one hand while the other held out a cellophane-wrapped bouquet of red roses, long-stemmed buds with a dewy look.

Anna was dumbfounded, until the landlady commented maliciously, 'Got yourself a rich boy-friend at last, have you? You didn't come home last night, did you? Oh, I noticed, went up and banged on your door a couple of times. Thought you were hiding because you didn't have the rent, but I suppose you were out earning it.'

Anna's face stiffened and burned. Carrying the roses, she turned on her heel.

'There's a note in there!' Mrs Gawton threw after her, her voice making it clear that she had read it. Anna didn't look back or answer, she went up the stairs, and Mrs Gawton stared after her, before vanishing into her own quarters.

In her room, Anna fished out the note with shaky fingers. 'Will be away for a few days. See you first night,' it said, his initials scrawled under the words.

Anna's emotions were confused but powerful: fury with him for sending the flowers and for believing that after what he had done to her she would want to see him again, painful relief because he had gone away and she wouldn't have to worry about finding him waiting for her outside the theatre, and a peculiar ache whose causes she preferred not to track down.

She was tempted to throw his flowers away so that they should not keep reminding her of him, but they were too beautiful, and she had never been given red roses before. She hunted out a chipped glass jug and filled it with water, arranging the roses in it tenderly, her fingertips brushing their cool petals. All evening she looked up and saw those deep red, satiny petals —and each time she thought of Laird, besieged by images of him. In a few short hours she had learnt so much about him; she felt as if she had always known him. That odd sensation of familiarity disturbed her. He was as insidious as spring, creeping up inch by inch while you weren't watching.

The problem was that she had started to like him very much; all that evening in his penthouse suite she had been registering aspects of Laird and liking what she noticed—his humour, his kindness, his arguments with that old man whom he had rescued from the gutter, his liking for the same poetry as herself, his teasing eyes and deep, cool voice.

None of that seemed to fit with what happened later, with Laird's ruthless use of her when she was too drunk to know what was going to happen.

Each time she thought of it she felt a pang of shame. It was ironic that she had been so worried about Patti—she should have worried about herself. If she had been more careful there wouldn't have been any consequences.

That was when it dawned on her that there was one possible consequence she hadn't taken into account.

She went white, sitting up with a hand over her mouth as if to silence the groan she gave. What if she was pregnant?

That idea kept her awake half the night, and she overslept and had to run to catch her bus without having time to eat. She bought a roll at a baker's and ate that when Joey gave them a coffee break, but she was so obsessed with her new fear that people kept looking at her oddly, and Dame Flossie actually asked her outright.

'What's wrong, dear? Not too well? Or just tired?'

Anna dragged a smile into her face. 'We're all tired, aren't we?' She made it light, but Dame Flossie's keen old eyes were shrewd as they studied her pale face, and even Joey seemed concerned.

'I hope you're not coming down with some bug, Anna,' he said impatiently. 'That's all I need.'

Anna imagined the way he would look if she was pregnant—how could she face that? She spent twenty-four miserable hours wondering what she would do if the worst proved true, and then her period started dead on time and for the first time in her life she welcomed it with deep, unutterable relief. At least she didn't have that to worry about! Not that it would have bothered Laird Montgomery at all—hadn't it occurred to him that he might get her pregnant?

He probably thought she must be on the Pill, Anna told herself grimly. Many girls were these days, but it had never occurred to Anna because she didn't sleep with anyone, she never had. Her life had been too hectic for there to be any room for men.

During the following week, she had little time for thinking about Laird, however. Joey's urgency drove them all from the minute they walked on to the stage to the minute they emerged, drained and weary, into the night air. The dress rehearsal was a total madhouse, everyone in a state of nerves, shaking like aspens, and Joey one second shouting with rage, the next becoming icy and remote as he bit out sentences that left them cringing.

Even Dame Flossie became a little overwrought and forgot a cue, and shortly after that Joey relented and sent them all home, telling them quite gently to relax and forget the play for a few hours.

'We've found all the flaws, I think, and done something to put them right,' he said, his face wry. 'Just make sure you remember everything I've said and we'll have a triumphant first night.'

Anna woke up several times that night, sweating with terror after dreaming that she'd dried up or tripped over a chair, and once that she found herself in the wrong play, acting among a cast of total strangers who kept giving her cues she had never heard before!

'Absolutely classic, my dear!' said Dame Flossie next evening when Anna mentioned her dream. 'We've all dreamt that one. I once dreamt I was Juliet and the rest of the cast were from *Hamlet,* but that wasn't as bad as dear old George Skillicorn—he dreamt he was playing Iago and suddenly realised the play was *King Lear,* then woke up and realised it wasn't a dream. Poor Georgie drank too much towards the end, I'm afraid. Mind you, the audience didn't seem to notice, it was a very thin house that night, thank God.'

Chuckling in her dressing-room, Anna asked Patti, 'Did you believe that?'

'It was funny,' Patti said uncertainly. 'But . . . who was George Skillicorn? I've never heard of him.'

'I suspect Dame Floss made him up. Either that or he was someone she knew when she was very young.' Anna looked into her mirror, her eyes had a hectic glitter to them. 'I'm so nervous I could scream!'

Patti was white under her make-up. 'Don't! I daren't even think about it. I know I'll go blank the minute I hear my cue.'

Patti didn't, of course, and Anna's nerves vanished the minute she was out of the wings and swallowed up into the electric storm of the play. She forgot the audience and herself; she was only conscious of what was happening on stage—and then her first laugh came and she almost went to pieces with surprise. From the dark auditorium faces swam out, eyes gleamed like fireflies. She caught Dame Flossie's commanding gaze and pulled herself together, carrying on. The next laugh came patly, where Joey had taught her to expect it, and the timing she had been so sure she would never get right came smoothly, she felt the pull on the line between herself and the audience. She played them effortlessly; loving their laughter, their held silence during the poignant moments of the play.

Afterwards she felt like a balloon whose string had been cut; she floated around, laughing, exchanging compliments and memories of the last two hours, her ears still ringing with the applause which had seemed deafening as they took the curtain calls.

They all knew it had worked; the play was a success. They didn't need to wait for the reviews in the morning papers or the flood of calls at the box office. Joey was smiling from ear to ear; Dame Flossie's dressing-room was crammed with admirers who filled the room with flowers, opened champagne, spilled out into the corridor and stared at the rest of the cast as they hurried by on their way to the first night party being held at a nearby restaurant.

Anna was talking to Joey Ross when she saw Patti with Laird Montgomery. Laird had bent his dark head; he was kissing Patti.

'We're bound to move into the West End now,' Joey said, but Anna barely heard him; she was watching Patti throwing her arms around Laird's neck and her body was icy with shock.

CHAPTER FOUR

JOEY'S voice halted as he realised she wasn't listening to him, he followed her gaze and exclaimed cheerfully, 'Laird! Hello! You got back in time, then—that's great. Did you enjoy it?'

Anna had never been so angry in her life. She would have walked away before Laird and Patti joined them, but under the mocking inspection of those grey eyes she held her ground, her chin lifted in defiance. She wasn't giving him the satisfaction of imagining that she was running away from him.

Behind stage was so crowded that Laird and Patti had to push their way through to Joey and Anna, and that gave time for Anna to note that Laird had his arm around Patti's slender waist and she was leaning slightly on his shoulder, the intimacy undisguised and so casual that Anna ground her teeth in bitter distaste, wishing she had never made such a fool of herself as to offer the other girl advice Patti clearly did not need and must have laughed over once she was alone.

She could hardly doubt the evidence of her own eyes, yet she was incredulous, nevertheless. How could Patti have deluded her so easily? She must be a better actress than Anna had believed; her performance as a shy, embarrassed adolescent had been superb. She had been totally convincing.

'Congratulations, Joey,' drawled Laird, shaking hands with him. 'A marvellous production.'

Oh, absolutely, Anna thought—Patti had given a brilliant performance and not in the play tonight.

'You had us all eating out of your hand,' Laird said, smiling. He was in evening dress; it infuriated Anna to see how breathtaking he looked in the elegant, expensively tailored suit. There was a red carnation in his buttonhole, and she stared at it, remembering the red roses he had sent her, her throat raw with pain and rage. Her dilated eyes slid up over his broad shoulders and that hard-boned face to find him watching her with insolent amusement.

'Especially you, Miss Rendle,' he murmured, taking a step towards her, his arm relinquishing Patti's waist. His hand came out and before Anna realised what he meant to do he had seized her own hand and was lifting it to his lips.

Her fingers shook as she felt the touch of his mouth on her skin, and he shot her a glance from under dark lashes, aware of that betraying tremor.

'You have a very rare gift,' he said. 'You can make people laugh *and* cry all at the same time. I can't remember a more exciting first performance in the theatre, can you, Joey?'

Joey smiled paternally. 'She has possibilities,' he conceded, without going over the top. 'If she works hard,' he added even more cautiously, then glanced at Anna with curiosity. 'I didn't realise you knew Laird, Anna.' His eyes narrowed as she flushed, then he laughed. 'Oh, of course, Patti must have introduced you—I'd forgotten you two had become friends.' Looking back at Laird, he asked quizzically, 'Is the cat out of the bag or do you still prefer to be anonymous?'

'Oh, I don't think we should let anyone else in on the secret,' drawled Laird, shrugging.

'Up to you,' Joey said indifferently. 'Are you coming to the party?'

'I wouldn't miss it for worlds.'

Anna's heart sank; if he was coming to the party she wasn't going to enjoy it—how could she? Quite apart from the nerve-racking tension of seeing him, remembering what he had done to her, she would have to watch him chasing Patti.

I'm not jealous, she told herself angrily. Patti must be out of her mind after what I told her—or did I merely make her twice as intrigued? Patti was only eighteen and fascinated by men like Laird Montgomery.

I should have remembered, Anna thought, silently furious with herself. At that age I was always reading about men like him and wishing I could meet one, a modern Lord Byron—mad, bad and dangerous to know. She had grown out of that phase, but Patti was still young enough to be vulnerable to Laird Montgomery, and he seemed interested enough in her. After all, he'd been waiting for *her* the night he took Anna to the penthouse, it had been Patti he was chasing!

A wave of heat swept over Anna as it dawned on her that he couldn't really have cared who he took to bed that night. He had wanted Patti but, cheated of her, he had taken Anna instead, like someone idly picking a flower on a walk and chucking it away a moment later.

Feeling sick, she swallowed, looking down, wishing bitterly that it hadn't happened, that she had taken the bus as usual that night. Laird Montgomery and his penthouse and his Rolls Royce might spell glamour to Patti, but he was despicable; he used his money and the power it gave him to get hold of young girls like Patti. No doubt that was what attracted him to the theatre, that explained why he had backed this play.

Dame Flossie darted up, incandescent with excitement, and threw her arms around Anna. 'You were wonderful, a joy to work with, your timing was perfect tonight,' she told her kissing her cheek.

Glowing at the accolade, Anna hugged her back, the ice around her heart briefly thawing. 'Thank you, you were wonderful too, I had tears in my eyes during that last scene and I distinctly heard sniffs from the front row.'

'Oh, so did I, my dear,' Dame Flossie agreed. 'And I opened my eyes and had a little peek, but she wasn't crying—it was a cold. She'd been blowing her nose all night.'

Anna laughed helplessly. 'Well, my tears were absolutely genuine. You were so marvellous!'

'You changed the business with the Chinese fan,' said Joey. 'Why did you lean against the fireplace, Dame Floss?'

She gave him a wicked smile, her eyes apologetic. 'Joey, I had the most appalling itch right in the middle of my back and I couldn't very well scratch it while the paying customers watched, so . . . '

Joey chuckled. 'So you leant on the fireplace and scratched on that?'

Anna laughed, too, but she was aware of Patti standing on tiptoe to whisper in Laird's ear. Dame Flossie glanced at them, too; what was she thinking? Those shrewd old eyes gave no indication.

'Well, if we're going to join the others at this party we should be making a move now,' Joey said, looking at his watch.

The backstage area had almost emptied of people without Anna realising it. She picked up her jacket from the chair on which she had thrown it half an hour earlier and was about to put it on when she felt Laird move behind her. His hand took the jacket and Anna tensed as he held it so that she could slip her arms into the sleeves. Typically, she couldn't manage it for a second or two, fumbling helplessly, very flushed, but at last he drew the jacket up over her slim shoulders and his hands lingered there, deliberately holding her, his fingertips moving softly, pressing down into her flesh. She intensely felt him behind her, his body not quite touching hers, and was angry with herself for being so aware of him.

Over her head, he suddenly asked: 'What did you think of my little sister, Dame Flossie?'

Anna's whole body jerked with shock. She looked incredulously at Patti, whose blue eyes hurriedly met hers, pleading apology in them, then fell from Anna's angry stare.

'A very nice little performance,' Dame Flossie said gently. 'In time I think she'll make a good actress, but she really ought to spend some time at a good drama school. Some actresses know by instinct what to do, some have to be taught. All of us can learn something from good teachers.'

'Oh, I'd love to go to drama school—I only wish my parents were here to listen to you!' Patti said eagerly. 'They don't want me to go on the stage, they wouldn't let me train.'

Anna had pulled away from Laird's hands and was walking angrily towards the exit. She didn't want to hear any more. They had made a fool of her, why had they lied? Why hadn't Patti told her the truth? Why all the secrecy?

Laird caught up with her in the street. As he grabbed her arm, Anna turned on him like a spitting wildcat. 'Leave me alone!'

'Not until we've had a little chat!' he said, tight-lipped as he watched her. 'OK, you're angry because Patti didn't tell you I was her brother. Surely you can see why? I'm backing the play—she was afraid the cast would think she'd got her part through me.'

'Can you blame them if that's what they think?' Anna muttered, her green eyes feverish. 'She was good enough in the part, but I can think of dozens of actresses who would have been as good, and a lot who would have been better.'

'It isn't true, though,' Laird said tersely.

'Maybe not, but they'd have believed it, and they wouldn't have been very friendly towards her.'

'That's why we kept it quiet, why she gave her mother's maiden name instead of her own. Look, Anna, Patti needed to prove she could act—not to me or herself, but to her parents. They didn't believe it, they wouldn't hear of drama school. I think they blame me for Patti's obsession with theatre—I've always been a theatre buff, this isn't the first play I've backed. So far my investments have always paid off, I pick them very carefully. When Joey Ross asked if I'd put up the money for this play I asked him to dinner to talk it over. That's how he met Patti, and she asked Joey if there was a part for her, it was a joke . . . '

'Oh, sure,' Anna said cynically, and he frowned.

'I tell you it was a joke! Joey laughed, we all laughed. I put up the money and it was weeks later that Joey offered her a part. He already had my promise of the money, he didn't need to do that.'

Anna pulled free and walked on across the road towards the restaurant at which the party was being held. Dame Flossie and Patti and Joey were coming behind them now; Anna heard their voices and laughter and wished she found something amusing in this situation. She wanted to be walking on air tonight—it should have been the biggest night of her life. Instead she felt angry and miserable.

'I don't like being lied to!' she threw at him, but she knew that what was really eating away at her was the thought of her warning to Patti about him. Patti had let her say all that without giving her the tiniest hint that she was making an idiot of herself.

'It was only a white lie,' Laird said defensively, frowning. 'Anna, you won't tell the others, will you? Don't ruin Patti's evening.'

Anna gave him a bitter smile. 'Oh, of course not! I wouldn't dream of doing that!' It didn't matter, apparently, that between them they had ruined *her* evening—*she* wasn't important. Staring into his eyes, she saw no flicker of awareness there, no memory of the night they had spent together. It had meant nothing to him, Anna thought, her stomach churning with pain and anger. She had been just one of many, and afterwards he had sent her red roses and wiped her from his mind.

'Patti's very fond of you,' Laird said. 'Your opinion matters to her.'

'Does it?' Anna wondered what Patti had made of those revelations about Laird, or hadn't they been any surprise to her? She must know her brother well enough to have some idea of his love life. Why didn't she tell me? Why did she let me go on and on . . . Anna was so angry she was shaking with it, but at that moment Patti came running after them, her eyes anxiously meeting Anna's.

'Don't be angry,' she pleaded, an uncertain smile on her mouth.

'Wouldn't you be, in my shoes?' Anna asked, but, face to face with Patti, felt the black rage dying out inside her and a rueful impatience taking its place. Patti looked like a child with her big blue eyes and anxious smile.

The others caught up with them before Patti could answer, and Joey opened the door and waved them through. The rest of the cast were waiting, their eyes on the door as they sat around a table, drinking champagne. They grinned and waved at the two girls, but Dame Flossie's entrance got the cheer, everyone stood up and clapped her and she swept over there, smiling benevolently, accepting their homage with her usual warmth.

Anna slid in between two members of the cast and avoided looking at Laird as they ate the supper laid on for them. She wasn't very hungry; her nerves on fire as they waited for the newspapers and the first reviews.

The assistant stage manager rushed in with them much later and everyone crowded round Joey as he hunted through the pages.

Anna was so tense her stomach was tied in knots, then Joey began to read the first review, and Anna felt her face burn at what it said about her. The others were more or less the same; Dame Flossie always took the lion's share of the praise, but Anna was singled out from the rest of the cast for special mention every time, and as Joey stopped reading Dame Flossie turned and kissed her.

'What did I tell you, my dear?'

'It's nice to have something to stick in my scrapbook, anyway,' Anna said, her eyes brilliant. 'My only other notice said I made a very sexy mushroom, which isn't quite how I want to be remembered by posterity.'

'Don't take too much notice of notices, though, my dear, they stunt your growth!' Dame Flossie told her.

Patti shyly leaned over and congratulated Anna. She was obviously unsure of her welcome, and Anna with a wry smile pushed her own anger aside and hugged her.

'You got a nice mention, yourself.'

'One line!' Patti said, going pink.

'Don't knock it, it's a start!'

Glowing with relief, Patti giggled. 'Well, I'm glad I didn't get any bad notices, anyway. Maybe now my parents will come and see the play. They were too nervous to come tonight in case I made a complete hash of it.'

The restaurant was empty now, except for the company, and the band Joey had engaged began to play. The cast began dancing on the little square of parquet which served as a dance floor. Anna danced with the assistant stage manager, talking cheerfully to him while out of the corner of her eye she observed Laird dancing with Patti.

Discovering that he was Patti's brother, not her lover, didn't alter the way Anna saw *him;* she wasn't prepared to forgive and forget as far as Laird was concerned. He had got her drunk and seduced her knowing very well that stone cold sober she wouldn't have let him lay a finger on her. That was despicable—and so was he! No doubt Patti had repeated to him what Anna had said about him; the two of them must have found it very amusing, the idea of Anna warning her against her own brother! Oh, yes, it must have been a great big joke, thought Anna, her teeth grating. What fun they must have had!

She danced with several other members of the company, including Joey, carefully avoiding being anywhere near Laird when the music stopped, and once, when he came purposefully towards her, moving just as firmly towards the powder-room in time to escape him.

Patti joined her there a moment later, eyeing her warily in the wall mirror as they both renewed their make-up.

'OK, don't give me that panda stare,' Anna said wryly. 'I forgive you, you don't have to apologise again.'

Patti laughed, but caught her lower lip between her teeth in obvious hesitation while she still looked at Anna with that uncertain expression.

'About Laird . . . ' she began, and Anna broke in roughly.

'No, I don't want to discuss your brother. We've already discussed him once too often, and I'm in no hurry to make a fool of myself again.' She had intended to keep her temper, but the rage bubbling inside her wouldn't be kept out of sight; it forced its way to the surface, her green eyes glittering as the hot words erupted. 'You told him, didn't you? Repeated all my lurid warnings about his intentions—my God, that must have made him laugh! What a lot of fun for both of you!'

'No!' protested Patti, her reflection in the mirror wide-eyed and distressed, or was she acting? Anna no longer knew. 'I didn't repeat anything you said, Anna, honestly!'

'Honestly?' Anna threw back in derision. 'Please! I wish I could believe what you said, but after all the other lies, that isn't easy!'

'I'd have been embarrassed, talking to Laird about it,' Patti stammered, her face carrying a sort of conviction. 'He's so much older than me. I know he's my brother, but he hasn't actually lived with us for years, he moved out when he was married . . . '

'Married?' Anna repeated hoarsely, staring at her; a deep, aching pain behind her eyes. The first time she met Laird, she had wondered if he was married—cynically, she had decided that no man that attractive could possibly have stayed single into his mid-thirties. Her suspicions about him had faded into the background after the night she spent at his penthouse—she had been too busy hating him for other reasons.

'It didn't last,' Patti said. 'His wife had affairs with other men, and Laird divorced her. It made him very cynical about women.' She looked away, very pink. 'When you told me about . . . about him making a pass at you the night he gave us a lift, I wasn't surprised. I knew he played around quite a bit, but don't take him seriously, Anna.'

'I've no intention of taking him seriously! Why do you think I gave *you* the gypsy's warning?'

'Yes, but . . . ' Patti looked at her uneasily. 'He can be very charming. I've heard my parents talking about it. My father's upset because Laird shows no sign of getting married again, Daddy gets cross when he hears Laird has been seen at parties with yet another woman, because it always comes to nothing. Don't get involved with him, Anna!'

Anna was burning with temper by now. 'I just told you I won't!' Had Laird told Patti about their night together? She couldn't meet the other girl's eyes, but curiosity was nagging at her. 'What was his wife like?' she asked, furious with herself for needing to know.

'I was only nine at the time—I barely remember Merieth.'

'Merieth? Was that her name? I've never heard it before.'

'I think it's Celtic. She was Welsh, anyway—very beautiful, with long black hair and a lovely face, but my parents never liked her. They thought she was spiteful, sly, too; but maybe that's just what they say since the divorce. People do seem to talk with hindsight, don't they?'

Anna was thinking, her brows knitted. 'You were nine at the time of the divorce? That's a long time ago. Did she marry again?'

'Oh, yes, but . . . '

The door opened and Patti stopped talking, looking round as Dame Flossie came in, her quick, sharp eyes moving from one to the other.

'Now then, you two! Stop gossiping in here and come back and join the rest of us! You're not supposed to walk out of a party!' she scolded, pushing

Patti towards the door. Anna reluctantly followed them, still absorbed in what she had just been told about Laird. Patti's revelations had made it even more clear that the wisest thing to do about Laird Montgomery was to keep well away from him, and Anna meant to do just that in future, but that decision didn't stop her from thinking about him and realising that his attitudes towards women had been born out of how he had been treated by one of her own sex. Anna didn't excuse him on those grounds; the fact that he had been hurt by his wife was no good reason for deliberately setting out to use and hurt other women. Nevertheless, her anger ceased to be quite so volcanic, although her pride still throbbed with the bruises he had left on it.

She was about to dance with Joey when Laird stood up too, his hand reaching out for her.

Joey laughed, raising his brows. 'My turn, I think.'

Laird forced a tight smile, shrugging, and sat down again. Joey moved off with Anna, grinning down at her.

'I get the impression Laird fancies you. I suppose you know he's our angel? He backed the play and it looks as if his investment is going to pay handsomely, but I must say I was very grateful when he agreed to put up the money. Although I'd got Dame Floss lined up, the rest of the cast were newcomers and I was having trouble raising the money.'

'I hope you're not going to ask me to be nice to him!' Anna said tartly.

'As if I would!' Joey said, grinning. 'On the other hand, don't go out of your way to be rude to him!' He spoke lightly, but Anna sensed that he was half serious. It was never easy to raise money for a play, especially with an unknown cast. 'And don't tell anyone that Patti is his sister, will you?' Joey went on. 'I don't want any snide remarks flying about. I didn't give her that part because I wanted her brother's loot, it was a purely professional decision—I wanted someone very young and innocent, and she was perfect.'

'I believe you,' Anna said wryly. 'But it looks like a hell of a coincidence.'

'That's why I want you to keep your mouth shut!' he said. 'I'm surrounded by cynics.'

She couldn't get out of dancing with Laird next, especially with Joey watching her. Finding herself in his arms again sent a wild tremor along her nerves, made her eyes darken. He danced well; his long-legged body instinctively graceful as he drew her closer, his hand pressing into the small of her back. His cheek brushed hers as he murmured, 'I thought of you all the time while I was away. Did you think of me?'

'No,' Anna said icily, and his face drew back a little so that he could stare at her. She turned her head, showing him a rigid profile.

'Did you get my roses?' he asked, frowning.

'Yes.'

'Didn't you like them?'

'They were very beautiful, but you shouldn't have sent them.'

'Why not? I wanted to thank you for a wonderful evening,' he said, a smile in his voice as if he was teasing her. Anna's teeth met. She knew why he had sent them; he didn't need to underline the message. If he thought he was ever getting her into bed again, he could think again!

The music had stopped; Joey was clapping his hands for their attention and as all the cast turned their faces towards him, he said crisply, 'OK, kids—I'm calling rehearsal tomorrow at eleven-thirty. There are still one or two rough spots, I noticed. Off you all go, and thank you.'

Anna yawned, collecting her jacket, and looked around for the assistant stage manager who had promised to give her a lift home. There wouldn't be a bus running at this time of night.

She couldn't see him anywhere, but as she hurried after the rest of the cast, crowding out of the restaurant, talking and laughing, Laird blocked her path.

'Looking for the young man with bushy hair? He's gone—I told him I'd give you a lift.'

The cool, bland voice made the blood rush to her head. She stared at him, shaking with resentment.

'You did what?' she snapped, and saw heads turn, eyes staring. 'What makes you think you have the right to calmly walk in and countermand my arrangements without so much as asking me?'

'I was doing him a favour,' Laird informed her, eyes gleaming with mockery. 'Did you know he lives just a couple of miles from here and that to take you home he would have to drive six miles there and six miles back again? He was dead on his feet and only wanted to go home to bed, so I suggested I'd take you.'

Anna saw Patti standing near the door, anxiously watching. Taking a deep breath, she forced down her anger. She shouldn't have erupted like that; he wasn't getting to her again, from now on she was going to be calm and distant every time Laird was within a mile of her.

'Thank you,' she said frostily, handing him a polite, phoney smile, then swished past him and joined Patti without giving Laird another glance.

The blue and silver Rolls made short work of the distance into central London from the riverside; the narrow, shabby dock streets vanishing past and in their place the wider thoroughfares of Piccadilly and then Mayfair. Patti made polite conversation for a few minutes, then fell asleep, her head lolling sideways on the cushions. Anna stared out of the windows, yawning. The heating in the limousine made her sleepier by the second, but she was afraid of shutting her eyes.

Laird finally slowed at some traffic lights close to her home and glanced back at her. 'You'll have to direct me from here.'

'Straight on, the third turning on the left and then one to the right,' Anna told him flatly.

He pulled up outside the house five minutes later, got out and came round to open the rear door for her, his hand resting under her elbow as she slid out. Anna freed herself as soon as she was standing upright on the pavement.

'Thanks for the lift, goodnight.' Her curt tone didn't deter him from following her towards the gate of the house, and she snapped over her shoulder, 'I can find my own way now, thank you.'

The street was far too shadowy, no street light nearby made it possible for her to see his hard-boned face clearly, only his eyes glittering under the windswept black hair.

'Are you sulking because I didn't tell you Patti was my sister?' he murmured right in her ear, as she stopped to hunt for her front door key. The warmth of his breath on her lobe made her stomach clench, but she lifted her head, moving slightly so that he couldn't do that again.

'No.' She put the key in the lock and his hand covered hers; his skin warm and firm. Anna stared at that long-fingered, powerful hand and remembered it touching her with far more intimacy; the memory sent waves of shame and anger through her again.

'We have to talk,' Laird said huskily.

She threw his hand off and turned the key, and the door swung open. 'I'm not interested, Mr Montgomery,' she bit out sharply. 'I have other plans for my future; I don't want to get involved with you. Please, take Patti home, and stay away from me after tonight. You'll just be wasting your time if you don't.'

She walked rapidly into the house and without looking back closed the door in his face, not knowing how he had taken what she said and preferring not to know. She hadn't needed Patti's warning about his cynicism and the scar left by his marriage and the divorce that followed; Laird Montgomery carried his own warnings in his sophisticated, sensual, hyper-aware face. He wasn't a man to care about. He would hurt you; and Anna had no intention of letting him do her any more damage. He had done enough already.

CHAPTER FIVE

ANNA woke up with a start, her muscles at once tightening as she prepared to leap out of bed to hurry to rehearsals, then she heard the ringing of church bells and it dawned on her—it was Sunday! She didn't have to get up or catch a bus across London; she could stay in bed all day if she liked and be totally lazy. This was her first day's holiday for weeks.

Stretching, she linked her hands behind her head and wiggled her toes under the covers. What bliss! She would get up soon, have a leisurely breakfast and later maybe take a stroll through the park to watch the squirrels.

Her mind wandered idly over her plans for the day, then she frowned, remembering that last night she had met Patti's parents. They had finally been persuaded to see the play and had come backstage in the interval, looking dismayed as they noticed the squalor of the poky little dressing-room shared by three members of the cast, but smiling politely as they shook hands with Patti's colleagues.

Their appearance had given Anna a double shock—Hugh Montgomery was far older than she had expected, he had white hair and a stooping body and was clearly in his seventies—while his wife was much younger and couldn't be above fifty. Anna was not mathematically inclined, but even she at once suspected that Laird was not this woman's son, unless she had given birth to him when she was around fourteen or fifteen.

'So you're Anna,' Mrs Montgomery said, warmly smiling. 'We've heard all about you from Patti.' She was handsome rather than beautiful, a tall woman with the dark hair and blue eyes she had passed on to her daughter, her face calm, her manner kindly and level-headed.

'We're enjoying the play,' Mr Montgomery chimed in, leaning on the ivory-headed cane he carried. His leonine head bore a strong resemblance to Laird, so did the direct gaze of his pale eyes. 'Dame Florence is a good as ever, and you seem to me to have a very starry quality yourself, Miss Rendle.' He smiled and she flushed, feeling she ought perhaps to put a finger under her chin and curtsey.

'Thank you, sir.'

'What do you think of Patti, hmm?' he demanded under cover of a moment when his daughter was showing her mother a view from the peephole in the wings.

'She's very good . . . ' Anna had begun politely, only to be cut short by a raised finger, shaken at her with peremptory insistence. 'The truth, now! Can she act?'

'*Yes!*' she assured him, stressing the word.

His old eyes peered into her face. 'Not up to your standard, though, eh?'

'You can't honestly expect me to answer that . . . ' she demurred, laughing angrily.

'You just did, Miss Rendle,' he commented drily.

'Patti's still very young,' Anna began, and he patted her cheek, smiling at her.

'And you're so old, is that it? How old, I wonder? Twenty-one? Twenty-two? D'you really think that in a couple of years' time Patti will be able to act you off the stage the way you do her now?'

'I hope I do nothing of the kind,' Anna protested hotly. 'We're a team, the whole company, we aren't in competition. The star system is dead.'

His sardonic stare reminded her of his son so forcibly that she blinked. 'Is that why Dame Florence's name is neon-lit outside this theatre tonight?' he asked, and Anna could think of nothing to say in answer.

As they left, Mrs Montgomery turned to Anna and said, 'Will you come to lunch soon? I'll tell Patti to fix a suitable day. It's been a pleasure to meet you, Anna.'

Anna had said smilingly that she had enjoyed meeting them, and would love to come to lunch. She might not have so readily agreed if she hadn't remembered that Laird no longer lived with them and wouldn't be there. As she and Patti stood in the wings later Patti had given her a shy, wistful look. 'What did you think of them?'

'Your mother's charming and your father is amazingly like your brother,' Anna said at once, then gave her a searching stare. 'Laird isn't your mother's son, is he? She looks too young to have a son that age.'

'Oh, didn't I tell you?' Patti asked, laughing. 'I'm so used to thinking everyone knows! No, my father was married before and Laird's really my half-brother.'

Anna heard her cue and turned away at once, taking on her alter ego as she walked on to the stage,

at once sucked into the drama being played out and
forgetting everything else.

Now, though, she thought back over that brief
conversation, her sleepy contentment seeping away
as Laird shouldered his way back into her thoughts.

Had his mother died or had there been a divorce?
She didn't want to think about it; it was dangerous
to be too curious about the man, it kept him in her
mind when what she ought to be doing was forgetting all about him. It was infuriating that Laird
simply refused to be evicted; he kept coming back.
Like indigestion, she thought crossly.

The morning after the first night another couple of
dozen red roses had arrived. She had still been in bed;
Mrs Gawton had handed them through the door,
positively apoplectic with curiosity, and Anna had
shut the door on her excited questions and put the
flowers down to sit and stare in brooding preoccu-
pation.

What was Laird playing at? she had been asking
herself with foreboding. She vividly remembered his
expression the night before as he looked up at the
shabby house, his eyes distasteful, his mouth twisting.
Now he knew where and how she lived, he could see
how far outside his own milieu she moved—so why
was he sending her red roses? He thought she was a
cheap pick-up, obviously. He thought he could buy
her with a few flowers and a candlelight dinner. Anna
had felt like shredding the dark red, scented petals
and flinging them to the four winds. If he laid one
finger on her again she'd hit him so hard he wouldn't
stop bouncing for a week!

Irritated with herself because she seemed unable
to stop thinking about him, she made herself get up

and have a bath. She had to share the bathroom with everyone else on her floor. The water was always lukewarm and had a rusty tinge when it first came out of the tap, making a knocking, shuddering noise. The bathroom was draughty and usually had a cobweb or two in the corners. Anna was always finding huge black spiders in the bath. She hated touching them, so she shut her eyes and turned the taps on full to wash them down the plughole, only to be full of guilt over it afterwards.

Today she wasn't tempted to soak for long; she towelled herself hurriedly and padded back to her room to dress, but at the top of the narrow stairs she saw a dark figure looming.

She gasped before she recognised Laird; in the shadows he had a distinctly threatening height.

When it dawned on her that it was him her crazy pulses didn't calm down; to her anxiety they even quickened as her eyes ran over him. He looked so out of place in these shabby surroundings, his clothes far too expensive and his manner radiating too much assurance. Long-legged, tall, with that strong-boned face and coolly commanding eyes, he confronted Anna with a mocking little smile.

'How did you get in here?' she burst out, and from the bottom of the stairs heard Mrs Gawton's voice.

'I let him in, dearie. He said he'd come to pick you up to have lunch. Isn't it all right?'

Anna heard the intrigued note in her sly voice and bit her lip, angrily aware of Laird's sardonic amusement at her predicament. She couldn't bear to argue with him in front of her landlady; she didn't want to give Mrs Gawton even more fascinating gossip to pass on to all her neighbours.

'Yes, thank you, Mrs Gawton,' she said, raising her voice politely, then swung and opened her door.

Laird wandered past her without a word, and Anna winced as she closed the door, watching his eyes flick round the room, his brows shooting up.

'So this is where you live,' he said, and she saw the place through his eyes, wishing to heaven that she hadn't allowed him through the door. She hadn't made her bed yet; she moved over to pull the quilt over it, her face burning, conscious of him watching her, assessing her well-washed old blue dressing-gown, her damp red-gold hair, her threadbare blue slippers.

'What are you doing here?' she muttered, turning to face him reluctantly. 'I thought I told you . . . '

'My family are expecting you for lunch,' he interrupted smoothly, and Anna's lips parted in bewilderment.

'But . . . no, we didn't make any arrangement. They invited me casually for some day, but no date was fixed.'

'Are you doing anything else today?' Those fine black brows winged upwards and his eyes read her expression. 'No? Then if you'll get dressed we'll be on our way.'

'I can't,' Anna stammered, totally thrown. 'I haven't got anything to wear.'

He didn't laugh or tell her that that was a female cliché; he gave her a wry look, then walked over to the battered old wardrobe in one corner of the room, opened it and ran his eyes over the sparse contents. Anna ground her teeth. What was he thinking as he inspected her pathetic pretence of a wardrobe? The hair on her nape bristled; what business of his was it anyway? She was poor now, but one day she would be able to buy what she liked, go where she liked, and meanwhile she wasn't taking pity or contempt from anyone, least of all Laird Montgomery.

'Stop that! Go away!' she snapped, shaking with rage.

Taking no notice, he pulled down a simple black dress which she had had since her first year at drama school. Tossing it on her bed, he ordered curtly, 'Wear this!'

Anna's mouth was rigid with obstinacy. 'Please apologise to your parents for me, but I can't come.'

'Give me one good reason!'

She lost her temper. 'You know very well why! I'd be totally out of place, I don't belong among your sort of people . . . '

He regarded her with open derision. 'You little snob!'

Anna couldn't believe her ears. Incredulously, she stammered, 'Me, a snob? Oh, that's funny. Don't be ridiculous!'

'Inverted snobbery is just as damn stupid as the usual variety,' Laird drawled, then his hand shot out and she felt him untie the belt of her dressing-gown, which fell open before she could stop it. 'Do I have to dress you myself?' Laird's voice was husky; he was staring at the sensuous shimmer of her naked body under a fragile, clinging drift of white fabric.

Anna shakily dragged the dressing-gown together again, her skin heated, her pulses hammering with a peculiar mixture of shock, anger and worrying excitement.

'Didn't I make myself clear last time?' she demanded furiously. 'I thought I'd spelt it out in letters ten feet high! I don't want to see you, Mr Montgomery. I'm not for sale, I don't want your red roses, and there won't be any more candlelight dinners for two, in your penthouse or anywhere else! You'll never get me into bed again, so stop trying! You wouldn't have got me there the first time if you hadn't poured all that champagne into me and got me too drunk to know what I was doing!'

He listened without moving, his eyes narrowed, gleaming like deep cold water. 'Oh, you were very drunk,' he agreed softly, and Anna's teeth met.

'How can you be so cool about it?' she hissed through those clenched teeth. He had no conscience and no scruples, but what angered her most of all was her own unwilling awareness of a permanent, pulsing attraction towards him. That night in the penthouse she had met a man she increasingly liked; she remembered laughter and talk between them, moments when she felt totally at home with him, trusted him. How could she have been so fooled?

He considered her drily, his head to one side. 'Tell me, how much do you actually remember?' he enquired, and Anna looked at him in utter disbelief.

'My God, you really are a bastard, aren't you? What do you want—a cosy chat about old memories? All I want to do is forget it ever happened, I ever met you; I'm not standing around here reminiscing with you!'

He lifted a lazy hand to her face, his fingertips caressing, and she jumped as if she had touched a live wire.

'Get dressed, I'll wait downstairs,' he ordered, and when she opened her mouth to protest he laid his palm across it. 'No, not another word! My parents are expecting you, they liked you very much, and you'll be quite safe in their house, I promise you.'

'Your promises are worthless,' she muttered, frowning. She didn't know what to do; she was tempted to go because she had liked his parents and she was curious about them, about everything to do with Laird's background. Curiosity killed the cat, she reminded herself, watching him walk to the door. If she had any sense she would refuse to leave this room, but she knew with an angry, helpless frustration that she was going to obey him, get dressed and let him drive her off in his Rolls. Her curiosity was too strong to resist.

Once he was out of the room, she hurried over to bolt the door, and heard him pause on the top stair and laugh softly.

'Five minutes, then I'm coming back to get you,' he threatened, and Anna made a face at the door as she heard him run downstairs.

She picked up the black dress and held it against herself, staring at her reflection in the dressing-table mirror.

Hardly Dior, was it? But perhaps that was just as well! She wasn't trying to attract anybody, was she?

'Au contraire, chérie,' she told her reflection angrily, pretending not to notice the glitter in her eyes and her feverish colouring. 'You're crazy, you know,' she warned that unfamiliar, unrecognisable face. 'Playing with dynamite isn't a good idea!'

But what possible harm could there be in getting to know his parents a little better? Or in seeing their home, finding out more about Patti, even more importantly getting a free lunch, and, no doubt, an absolutely terrific one!

What would she do if she didn't accept? She had some cheese and eggs—a cheese omelette? And after lunch a bus ride to the Embankment and yet another wander around the Tate, admiring modern art and trying not to look too hard at the still life paintings because the grapes and apples made her feel so hungry!

She smoothed the little black dress down over he hips, frowning at the way it clung; the deep plunge of the neckline made her uneasy and she had forgotten how insistently it outlined every curve of her body. She brushed her hair until it glittered fiercely and did her make-up with great care, wishing she had something else to wear. Jeans were out of the question and her only decent skirt was at the cleaners; this would have to do, but it certainly didn't help her to merge into the background.

Looking out of the window, she saw it was a cool but bright spring morning—should she risk going out without a coat? She had a rather pretty jade and black striped velvet bolero left over from her days in rep. She rarely wore it, but it wouldn't look out of place with the black dress and at least it wasn't as shabby as her jacket.

If their play went into the West End she could buy herself some new clothes, she dreamed, leaving the room to join Laird in the Rolls. If, if, if . . .

Mrs Gawton was hovering in the hall. 'Going out, Miss Rendle? That's a beautiful car, I always say you can't beat a Rolls Royce. Going somewhere special, are you?' Her avid gaze flitted over Anna, who flinched in the face of that shameless curiosity.

'Out to lunch,' Anna said shortly.

'Oh, nice! And all these lovely write-ups you've been getting for your play, really coming up in the world these days, aren't you?'

Anna's smile hurt. She managed to get past Mrs Gawton and escape into the nice, clean air, taking a deep breath—the woman made no secret of what she was thinking, and Anna hated the sly speculation in her eyes.

Laird was just coming up the path; he halted as she came out. 'There you are! I said five minutes, not fifteen!' He slid an assessing glance over her from head to toe. 'Charming. I like the bolero; a stylish touch.'

Anna only wanted to get away from the house and the eyes she felt from behind the grimy lace curtains. She let Laird slide her into the front seat of the Rolls, staring straight ahead while he got behind the wheel and started the ignition. A moment later they were moving smoothly down the street.

'Will you be warm enough, though?' he asked with a sideways flick of the eyes.

'Yes, thanks,' she said shortly.

'What's the matter now?' he asked impatiently, putting his foot down so that the limousine shot forward with a stately roar.

'My landlady annoyed me,' she admitted with a rueful little grimace, because, after all, it wasn't his fault that Mrs Gawton had a disgusting mind. She had a suspicion that she was beginning to blame Laird Montgomery for everything that happened to her that she didn't like. Lowering her lashes, she watched him through them obliquely—he didn't look much like a scapegoat, but she was using him as one.

He had a striking profile, she observed a little dreamily; that strong bone structure, of course. The way the spring sunshine hit his cheek showed her how recently he had shaved; his skin was baby-smooth along his jaw.

'How long have you been living in that dump?' he asked, his heavy-lidded eyes hiding what he was thinking.

'Longer that I care to remember,' she sighed.

'I know a spacious, beautifully furnished apartment overlooking Green Park,' he murmured. 'A luxury block with maid service and a lift, full central heating, of course, an indoor swimming pool and jacuzzis . . . '

Her breath caught—she had never in her life felt such overpowing rage. It grew inside her like an erupting volcano, shooting flames and red-hot lava through her. She couldn't make a sound, staring at him, her hands screwed up into fists, and Laird watched her sideways as he drew up at traffic lights.

Anna couldn't believe it when she heard him laughing softly, his brows flickering upwards.

'You should see your face,' he drawled. 'Wasn't that the offer you were expecting? After what you said about not being for sale I got the impression you'd been waiting for a proposition, and I wouldn't want to disappoint you.'

'Get lost!' Anna snarled.

'Or you could move into the penthouse,' he continued as though she hadn't said a word.

If she hadn't been so angry she might have been curious to see how high he would bid for her. What was she worth? she wondered grimly. What was the going rate for a mistress these days? How many had Laird had?

That was when an odd thing happened. Her whole body seemed to switch off. It was a really weird sensation, and Anna did not enjoy it at all. Her heart had stopped, she wasn't breathing; she couldn't hear, her eyes were blind.

My God! I'm falling in love with him, she thought. Why else am I so jealous at the thought of other women in his arms?

Then her heart went on beating, she breathed raggedly, and heard Laird talking next to her in that amused voice.

'Your trouble is, you've got no sense of humour, or maybe you did too many Victorian melodramas when you were with that repertory company?'

He was only joking, Anna thought with sick relief, but she was in no state to find him very funny. Her mind was too busy processing her discovery——dealing with it like someone handling radioactive material——wearing protective clothing, at a great distance and very, very reluctantly.

She hated the thought of the other women he had had; her imagination worked overtime, flashing her pictures she didn't want to see, feeding her jealousy until it burned darkly inside her.

CHAPTER SIX

'YOU'RE not even listening, are you?' Laird asked, impinging on her thoughts and making her jump.

She looked round at him, her lashes fluttering down against her flushed cheek. 'Sorry, I was miles away—what were you saying?' She was proud of her level tone; it sounded very convincing and couldn't possibly give him a clue to what had been obsessing her for the last few minutes. She had worked her way doggedly to deciding that she was suffering from an old-fashioned case of chemical reaction; her stupid genes were playing up, that was all. Laird was physically attractive, why deny that? He'd made love to her and given her a craving for what she had had once and couldn't help wanting again. It was very simple, wasn't it? Laird was addictive. She would just have to fight it; cure herself.

'Never mind,' he said drily. 'We're almost there now.'

The Rolls had purred round a corner into one of London's large squares, and Anna looked casually out of the window, doing a double-take as she recognised the place.

'Wolfstone Square?' Her head swinging towards Laird, she stared accusingly. 'This is where you dropped Patti the other night!'

He slowed and parked outside the same large white façade, his mouth ironic. 'Sorry about the little deception . . . '

'Lie,' she corrected tartly. 'You and Patti lied to me—this isn't a hotel! I thought it was odd then; it didn't look like a hotel.'

Her eyes rose to skim over the building, mentally pricing it and grimacing. It had a solidly elegant authority; smooth portico, gleaming black and gold front door with a Georgian polished knocker, rows of nicely proportioned windows. It was big enough to make a hotel, anyway; at least a dozen bedrooms, surely?

'Now that you know why Patti couldn't tell you the truth, you must understand,' Laird said with an optimism she found annoying. He was so casual about it all!

'I still don't like being told lies,' she informed him coldly, reluctant to get out of the limousine and walk up those steps, then she saw the front door swing open and several figures framed in the doorway. One of them was a small, thin man in a dark suit—the other was Patti, and she came running down towards the parked Rolls.

Laird got out and came round to open the door for Anna, and Patti gave her a hug.

'Oh, I'm so glad you came, I was afraid you wouldn't.' She was wearing a blue and white striped sailor suit with a broad white collar, matelot bodice and a pleated blue skirt. 'Come and talk to Mummy, she's in the conservatory talking to the plants—she has this theory that they need to know you like them.'

Anna smiled. 'I've heard lots of people say that.' She let Patti pull her up the steps, past the man in the dark suit who was holding the door open.

'This is Jimmy, he and his wife run the house for us,' Patti told her as Anna looked uncertainly at him.

Jimmy gave Anna a polite inclination of the head, but said nothing in reply to her 'Hello.'

Laird was sauntering into the house behind them. He threw his car keys to the other man. 'Park it, will you, Jimmy? Thanks.'

Anna didn't look back, her eyes busily absorbing everything she saw, shaken by a new realisation of how different their life-style was from her own. The contrast was painful. Her dreams of wealth and fame had never been this concrete. The gleam of polished panelling, the oil paintings hanging on walls, the bowls of flowers everywhere and the magnificent furniture they passed made her even more self-conscious about her plain black dress and cheap shoes, but when they walked into the conservatory and Mrs Montgomery looked up her smile was immediate and very warm.

'Oh, there you are, Anna. How nice of you to come! Please, sit here—I was just going to ring for coffee, will you have some?'

Anna said she would love some and they sat in the leafy sunlight talking for quite a time; all around them potted plants whose tendrils swung or climbed, ferns in white glazed pots, rambling ivy, cacti and spring flowers. It was a pleasant place to sit; the air warm and scented.

'Lunch should be ready soon,' Mrs Montgomery said, glancing at her watch.

'I'll go and check,' offered Patti, jumping up in a flurry of vivid blue pleats. Her mother looked after her as she vanished, her skirt almost the colour of Mrs Montgomery's blue eyes.

'We weren't very happy about the idea of Patti going on the stage,' she murmured. 'I expect she told you that?'

'She did mention it,' Anna admitted carefully.

'Laird encouraged her.' Mrs Montgomery's mouth was impatient. 'He's always spoilt her, right from babyhood. Over-compensating, I think. He wanted to show me he didn't resent me, so he made a big fuss of my baby.' She smiled at Anna. 'Funny creatures, boys. He was at the awkward age when Patti was born—seventeen and shooting up like a beanstalk, every time I saw him he'd grown another inch. He was very vain at that age, though, and obsessed with how he looked.'

'You're fond of him,' Anna said, and the other woman laughed.

'Oh, of course! I knew I was too young to be a mother to him, but I was scared he would be jealous of me and his father, and Hugh was very fond of him, it would have been difficult if Laird had resented me. I didn't really know how to treat him, but he had surprising common sense, even then. He . . . set the tone, I suppose you could say. He treated me like a big sister, not a stepmother, and I took my cue from him.'

'What happened to . . . ' Anna bit the question off before it emerged, but Mrs Montgomery was quick.

'His own mother?' she guessed. 'Divorced, oh, years before I met Hugh. When Laird was quite small. I'm afraid she wasn't a very affectionate mother. In fact, I don't think she cared a damn about him.'

'Did he see much of her after the divorce?'

'Almost nothing. She went off to South America with the man she'd married, and she died out there —the climate didn't suit her. She had rather delicate health. I don't know how upset Laird was; children can hide things rather well. My husband tried to keep the boy with him as much as possible.' Mrs Montgomery smiled wryly. 'My husband believes in over-compensating, too! They were very close, and I tried not to come between them, I wanted us to be a family. Funnily enough, it was Patti who made us one in the end, although I'd been so worried about Laird's reaction.'

'I realised he was very fond of her,' Anna said, glancing down in brief embarrassment as she remembered her own suspicions about them. She could hardly tell Mrs Montgomery that she had believed Laird was trying to seduce Patti.

'They're fond of each other. It's entirely mutual, but I wish Laird wouldn't intervene between her and us. He made it easy for her to get into the theatre and I would have preferred it to be hard. How are we to know if she really has the stamina and the dedication to get anywhere if Laird hands her a part on a plate?'

Anna stiffened, her eyes fixed on the other woman's face. 'Is that what he did?' Laird had said that Patti had got the part without any help from him, Joey and Patti had insisted it was true—had they all lied to her?

'In a sense—he introduced her to that director —what's his name? Joe?' Mrs Montgomery's smooth brow wrinkled.

'Joey Ross?'

'Yes, Laird introduced Patti to the man and that's how she got the part. If Laird hadn't made sure she met him, the director wouldn't have thought of her, would he?' Mrs Montgomery looked impatiently at Anna. 'It's a very hard life for a girl, I'm sure you've found it so, Anna. So much competition and so few jobs . . . I wish you would tell Patti just what she'd be letting herself in for if she persisted with this silly idea.'

Anna looked at her gently, not wishing to argue with her, but feeling she must be honest. 'I've already told Patti quite a bit about the dreary side of the job.' She didn't add that Patti had seemed entranced by those little cameos of life in stage digs: grey provincial theatres, disgusting meals, arguments and feuds between the cast, everybody helping to move scenery or even paint it, outbursts of hysteria or wild laughter over accidents on stage.

'I really think she knows what sort of life it is,' she stressed, feeling sorry for the other woman. Mrs Montgomery was looking depressed; Anna's answer had not been what she wanted.

'How long do you think this play will run?' Mrs Montgomery asked gloomily, her mouth turned down at the edges.

'Ages, I hope,' Anna said, laughing. 'But, afterwards, don't you think that . . . ' She broke off, wondering if she ought to offer Mrs Montgomery advice. After all, they had only just met.

'Yes? Go on, Anna, what were you going to say?' The other woman looked eagerly at her.

'Well, the best possible training for the theatre is at one of the top London drama schools. If Patti went to one of them, that would give her time—three years of hard work, and believe me, they really drive you hard there! I know, I went to one—Patti would have plenty of time to work out whether she had the guts and the talent for the job.'

While Mrs Montgomery was digesting this, there was a step on the tiled floor and they both looked up to see Patti joining them.

'Lunch in five minutes,' she said, her eyes moving from one to the other. 'You've been talking about me,' she accused, her smile rueful.

'Is your father still in his study?' Mrs Montgomery asked, ignoring the accusation. 'I'll go and wake him up. He pretends to be reading the Sunday papers, but he's really having one of his catnaps.' She smiled at Anna, her eyes full of warmth. 'He keeps his energy level topped up with little naps every hour or so, but he'll never admit as much.'

When she had gone, Patti asked: 'What were you saying?' but Anna dodged the question, teasing her.

'It's a common delusion that people are talking about us when we aren't there,' she mocked, and from the doorway Laird laughed, making her jump. It infuriated Anna to feel her pulses racing at the sound of his voice; he had a disastrous effect on all her senses and she must do something about it, but what?

'Have you been talking about *me?*' he enquired lazily.

'Why on earth should we do that?' Anna retorted, shooting a sarcastic smile in his direction.

'Because I'm so fascinating?'

'Modest, too,' she murmured, eyes lowered.

'Oh, he's as vain as a peacock,' said Patti, giggling.

Anna didn't smile at that; she was wondering if it was true and then crossly asking herself why she should care, if it was. Laird was no concern of hers. Her only concern was herself and her stupid feelings for him, and the sooner she cured herself the better.

'There's no subject as interesting as ourselves,' Laird said with amusement, but it wasn't true, thought Anna, watching him as he picked a leaf from a plant and rubbed it between his fingertips to release a pungent lemony scent. There was one subject far more riveting than oneself—if you were in love, that was! Then, all you thought about, cared about, was the other person; they occupied every waking minute, a driving obsession making you want to find out everything you could about them.

It was a relief to Anna when they were summoned to lunch and she could concentrate on talking to Mr Montgomery for a while. He asked her endless questions about herself, the play, her reasons for wanting to be an actress. She felt a little as if she was in front of the Spanish Inquisition, although his voice was gentle and his smile benevolent. She could see why he had been a success in business; he had a genius for gathering detail and assimilating it.

Laird said little, but he watched and listened intently, his grey eyes hooded and unreadable.

Patti said nothing much, either, except when Anna answered one question about her family with the brief admission that she had none at all.

'Oh, Anna, I had no idea!' Patti burst out, her eyes distressed. 'I mean, I realised your parents were dead, but I didn't know you had no relatives at all.'

'You get used to it,' Anna replied tersely. When she was a child it had made her miserable, but it no longer bothered her quite so much. She had made work the centre of her life for years; work didn't fail you. It didn't die, either, nor could it hurt you.

The man called Jimmy whipped away her plate a moment later as she finished the last morsel of the delicate vanilla cream. The meal had been delicious, but under Mr Montgomery's grilling Anna hadn't enjoyed it quite as much as she would have done if she hadn't been so distracted.

They took their coffee in the drawing-room, then Mr Montgomery slowly made his way back to his study, leaning on his wife's arm, and Laird stood up, too, looking at Anna.

'Let me give you a guided tour of the house—I want to show you some theatre prints I bought last year.'

Anna gave Patti a quick look. 'Coming, Patti?' The last thing she wanted was to find herself alone with Laird.

As they were beginning to climb the wide, polished stairs, however, Mrs Montgomery came out of a room and called Patti. 'I won't keep her a moment, but we want to talk to her,' she apologised to Anna, who had halted.

'We'll start in the night nursery,' Laird told Patti as she went towards her mother. 'And work our way down from there—join us when you escape.' He grinned at his stepmother, who shook a reproachful head at him.

Anna reluctantly followed Laird up several floors. The thick carpet gave way to a more hardwearing variety, the stairs became narrow and badly lit. Laird pushed open a door on the very top floor and Anna looked around the small, square room. It had tiny windows which shed little light, an old brass bed occupied one corner and around the room, dozens of toys—a delightful Edwardian dolls' house completely furnished and with tiny occupants frozen in chairs, at tables, even in a bath; a battered old wooden rocking horse with a red leather saddle with real stirrups; a row of bears and stuffed toys; a wooden fort with soldiers and cannon arranged around it and some dolls with fixed glass eyes and faded dresses, all shapes and sizes from a demure Victorian in poke bonnet and many petticoats to a mass-produced doll wearing red trousers and a black leather jacket.

'Oh, how lovely!' exclaimed Anna, her eyes lighting up. 'But it's rather sad, as though it was all waiting for a child . . . '

'Patti was the last, she was much kinder to her toys than I was—I regularly broke them.' Laird walked over to the nearest wall. 'These are the old prints—there were some here already, but I added to them.'

Anna reluctantly dragged herself away from admiring the dolls' house and joined him. The prints were very funny; one or two were after Hogarth, wickedly libellous cartoons of famous actors. She wandered around, laughing, while Laird showed her each one, but her eyes kept moving back to the toys. As they halted by the rocking horse she put a hand on its threadbare mane, wistfully stroking it, and Laird watched her with a crooked little smile.

'He's called Dandy.' Suddenly his hands shot out and got her by the waist, and Anna gasped, staring up at him for one second before she felt her feet leave the floor.

The next minute she was on the rocking horse, riding side-saddle, with Laird setting the horse in motion.

'I'm too heavy for it!' she protested, but he wouldn't let her climb off.

'You were dying to have a ride, don't pretend you weren't.' His grey eyes were gently teasing. 'Some children are a bit older than others, that's all.'

She went pink, but couldn't deny that she had badly wanted to ride the old wooden horse with its staring eyes and dappled grey coat, the paint wearing thin, fading, but so gently that one felt it had been worn down with generations of loving arms and hands.

'My father kept all this stuff up here for my children,' Laird said, watching her rocking, her head now above his own. 'Now it will go to Patti's, I suppose.'

Anna looked at the red leather reins she was holding. 'You don't plan to have children?'

'It's unlikely.' His voice was flat and terse. There was a silence, then he said, 'I was married years ago, did Patti tell you?'

'She mentioned something,' Anna whispered, unable to meet his eyes in case he read her expression.

'My wife went off with one of my friends.' He laughed shortly. 'Some friend! He wasn't the first, though—Merieth wasn't faithful to me for long, we'd only been married a few months when I found out she was seeing someone else. We had a very nasty row and she promised to give him up. She did, but it wasn't long before there was another man, and another—it was a pattern. She had men like someone eating sweets, unable to stop. By the time she ran off with the last one I was glad to see the last of her. I was sick of knowing people laughed at me behind my back, sick of wondering which of my friends had had her.' He walked away to the window and stared out at the pale blue spring sky. 'I swore then that I'd never marry again.'

'Did you ever see her again?' Anna asked huskily.

'No. She died a few years ago—overdose, I gather. She was on drugs by then. Merieth had most of the vices, she was as weak as water.'

Anna stared at him, her eyes burning, absently aware of the power of his lean body in the beautifully cut suit. Something quivered inside her like a plucked harp string, a high, resonant note. Had he loved his wife very much? The bitterness in his voice suggested he had, and she grew angry with herself because it hurt to think about that. She had no right to be jealous of his ex-wife. If Laird was haunted by the other woman that was his affair. She swallowed, her throat rough, her skin icy. It was crazy stupidity to let herself care about him.

Whatever reason Laird had for being the way he was, the fact remained—he was cynical where women were concerned and determined not to commit himself to another one. Any woman who let herself care about him was asking to get hurt, and Anna was no masochist.

He turned suddenly, his face wry with self-mockery. 'Oh, to hell with it! I shouldn't have started talking about her, the subject always depresses me.' He closed his hands around her small waist and smiled into her eyes. 'Enjoyed your ride?'

'It was fun,' Anna said huskily, her breathing suddenly rapid.

Laird lifted her off the old rocking horse, his hands gripping her waist tightly, but he didn't put her down at once. He held her so that their faces touched and

gently kissed her mouth, his lips warm and searching.
Anna fought not to enjoy it; she kept her eyes open,
watching him, and saw his eyes had closed. He slowly
let her slide downwards, their bodies touching, then
he locked her close to him without taking his mouth
from hers and bent her backwards in the circle of his
arms. Anna's head began to swim, she clutched at his
wide shoulders to keep her balance, protesting in a
muffled way under his exploring mouth.

In her struggle, she moved too close to the little
brass bed, and suddenly realised it when the back of
her knees touched the side of it.

'Let go,' she muttered, wrenching her head backwards, and Laird looked down at her through half-
closed eyes, breathing hard.

'I think I hear Patti coming,' Anna lied, and he
laughed, his eyes wickedly amused.

'I can only hear your heart beating,' he mocked,
watching the heat flowing up her face to her hairline.

'Well, we ought to go down . . . '

'They won't be worried, this is a big house, we
could take hours to explore it.' He lifted a hand to
her ruffled red-gold hair, sliding his fingers through
it gently, combing the strands and letting them fall
again. 'Your hair's a fabulous colour,' he murmured.
'Like fire, like candle flames.'

She gave him a quick, disturbed look, remembering that candlelit dinner and what had followed
it, and Laird's grey eyes gleamed with enjoyment, the
thought flashing between them as if they could read
each other's minds, and Anna thought with a pang
of misery that she often felt she could read his
thoughts, they had a telepathic link, only to be
plunged into uncertainty when a shutter went up

between them. Laird could shut her out of his mind, but she wasn't quite so sure that she could exclude him from hers. He seemed to know far too much about her.

'I wasn't entirely joking, Anna,' he said suddenly. 'In the car, when I offered you a flat—you really should get out of that filthy little room. It's no fit place for you. I hate seeing you in it. Why don't you let me take care of you?'

Her face turned white. 'No,' she said in a low, hoarse voice.

'I'm trying to be straight with you, Anna,' he said quickly. 'I've told you why I don't believe in marriage, but that doesn't mean you can't trust me to take care of you. I want to look after you, Anna.'

'I can look after myself!' She pushed at his shoulders, frowning angrily. She was afraid he would see how much he had hurt her by the offer; he mustn't realise she was vulnerable to him, he would only take advantage of that.

'You haven't made much of a job of it so far!' he retorted, looking impatient.

'I think I've made a damn good job of it,' Anna said, resenting that. 'I have a roof over my head, just about enough money and a job with an exciting future—lots of people would think I was lucky! And I haven't been reduced to selling myself yet.'

'That wasn't what I meant!' he snapped, his face dark red.

'Wasn't it?'

'No, it damn well wasn't. I'm not trying to buy you. I just suggested that your life might be a lot easier if you let me take care of you. Why shouldn't we live together? Hundreds of other couples do it every day, why shouldn't we?'

'Maybe because they're in love,' Anna said bleakly. 'And we're not!'

He stared at her, his eyes glittering. 'In love? What does that mean, anyway? Wish-fulfilment, fairytale endings, delusion! I thought you had more sense than that. I don't want you making me promises you won't keep, nor will I make them to you—but I'm a rich man and I can do a lot for you. I enjoy being with you, you're good company and I find you physically attractive—isn't that a better basis for living together than a lot of empty words about being in love for ever? At least I'm honest when I tell you what I feel.'

'That's just it,' Anna said bitterly. 'You don't feel anything.'

His mouth went crooked and a gleam came into his eyes. 'Oh, no, you're wrong,' he said huskily, and she trembled at that look, backing away from him, forgetting that the bed was so close. She gave a little wail as the back of her knees hit the edge of the bed, and couldn't regain her balance in time. Laird laughed softly at her startled expression and a second later was on the bed with her, his mouth hunting for hers. Anna didn't have time to think; a wave of instinctive feeling hit her as his kiss parted her mouth, and she went down under it, drowning in passion.

Her eyes shut, she abandoned herself to the wild, erotic sensations he was arousing in her; his lips on her throat, her eyes, moving down between her breasts, their sensuous invitation making her dizzy. She lost all idea of time, all common sense.

'Now tell me I don't feel anything,' Laird mocked softly, lifting his head a long time later, and she lay on the bed, drowsily opening her eyes to look at that hard-boned, triumphant face.

As the desire drained out of her, she grew cold and miserable, realising what a fatal mistake she had made, betraying herself to him, letting her body command her mind. Laird's mocking little smile was like a knife in her heart; he thought he had won.

'That isn't emotion,' she whispered shakily. 'That's chemistry. There's nothing special about it; you could have the same pleasure from any one of dozens of women, it doesn't mean a thing. And that isn't good enough for me. I want more from a man than sex.' She freed herself without difficulty, Laird's hands dropping away at once. Sliding off the bed, she ran her hands over her ruffled hair and walked unsteadily to the door, looking back at him from there, her chin up. 'The answer's still no, Mr Montgomery, and it always will be.'

He lay there, staring at her, his dark hair spilling over the pillow and his lean body sprawled casually on the bed, but he didn't answer, and Anna turned and went out.

She met Patti on the stairs and together they looked at the rest of the great house, but while Anna admired furniture and gently touched beautiful objects she was aching with compassion for Laird. He had offered her desire, a sensual delusion, a sating of the senses—but no love, and she would have starved in the streets rather than accept. He hadn't offered her love because he had none to give; he had once been hurt and he was determined never to love anyone again. Laird must be very lonely and emotionally in deep freeze; he wouldn't want her pity, but he had it.

CHAPTER SEVEN

ANNA did not expect she would ever see Laird again. He drove her back to her dingy little flat in a cool silence a few hours after that argument in the old nursery of his home, and she saw from the rigid planes of his face that he was angry with her for turning down his proposition. She could guess from that expression just how he looked to the directors of a company which had the temerity to reject an offer from him. Over lunch he and his father had talked about some firm Laird had wanted to take over but which was giving him a fight.

'I'll get them, don't worry,' Laird said through his teeth, scowling. 'And when I do, that board is out on its collective ear.'

Anna had looked down, her nerves jumping at his expression, feeling sorry for the directors he intended to fire, but now she felt far more sorry for herself. She didn't imagine Laird was mentally planning reprisals against her, but she hated to meet the cold, distant grey eyes and know that she was unlikely to be seeing him in future.

'Thanks for the lift,' she muttered as she got out of the Rolls. 'Goodnight.'

She almost said 'Goodbye', and the look Laird gave her made her feel that he had heard the word even if she hadn't said it. He drove off with a smooth snarl and Anna let herself into her flat a moment later, looking with distaste around the shabby room.

The contrast with the house she had just left was painful, but she still wasn't tempted to accept Laird's offer. He had talked about caring and looking after her, but he hadn't promised to love her, and without that the rest was worthless. After all, what would it cost him to give her a luxury flat, with or without a jacuzzi? He ran one of the biggest building firms in the country; he had probably built the whole damned luxury block of flats. It was easy for him to spend money; loving cost more.

She lay in bed later, brooding over him, and grimly eyeing the four square walls which held everything she owned. Now, if he had offered to move in here with her, that would have been a gesture of love! she thought—and then began to giggle helplessly at the very idea of Laird living in what he had contemptuously called 'that dump'.

She went to sleep that night fiercely determined to forget she had ever met him. It shouldn't be too hard—after all, her feelings towards him were very new, they should be easy to uproot, their roots could only be shallow.

Next morning she left at half past ten to get to the theatre by eleven-thirty for a rehearsal which ended at one o'clock, in time for the cast to have lunch and go home for a rest, until they had to get back to the theatre for the evening performance. They were getting into a routine now as they settled down to six evening performances a week, plus the Saturday matinee. Joey called the occasional rehearsal to keep their performance fresh and make sure they didn't slide into giving any less than their best but, that apart, they were all locked into the strange life-style which being in a long run meant. Getting up late, having a leisurely breakfast and doing the shopping and the housework before lunchtime, and afternoons which passed too rapidly and ended with an hour or two lying on her bed until it was time to go to the theatre; that was Anna's day now.

When she saw Patti at rehearsals she got a quick, friendly smile which was subtly different; they had been friendly for a long time now, but meeting Patti's parents, spending a day at her home, had made them friends. They had got to know one another away from the theatre. Yet Anna felt uncomfortably that it could never be a real friendship until Patti knew as much about the way *she* lived as Anna now knew about Patti's background. A one-sided intimacy was no intimacy at all.

'Come and have lunch with me one day this week,' she said lightly, later, as they were walking out of the theatre at the end of the rehearsal.

Patti looked surprised but nodded amiably. 'Love to—where?'

'My place,' said Anna, not caring to dignify the room with the description 'home'.

'When?' Patti asked, and they fixed a day and time, and Patti wrote down the address. Anna told her the name of the nearest underground station, but Patti said she would probably come by car. 'I'll get Jimmy to drive me over,' she said. 'Then you and I can go to the evening performance together, can't we?'

'Jimmy?' Anna repeated, puzzled.

'You met him at our house, remember?'

The penny dropped and Anna nodded. 'Oh, of course—your butler.' The name hadn't impinged on her consciousness.

'Well, he's more than that,' Patti told her, laughing. 'He does all sorts of things—he and his wife run the whole house, I don't know what we'd do without them.'

The following Friday Anna waited rather nervously for Patti to arrive, afraid of her reaction when she saw where Anna lived. It was impossible to cook a complicated meal on the electric ring which was all Anna had; so she had prepared a vegetable soup followed by salad. The room was tidy, but Anna kept remembering the splendour of Patti's home and wishing grimly that she hadn't invited her here.

At noon she began watching from the window for Patti's arrival; dead on a quarter past twelve the blue and silver Rolls came into sight, and Anna stiffened, trying to see the face of the driver. It wasn't Jimmy. It was Laird who got out of the driver's seat and came round to help Patti alight. His eyes shot upwards and Anna hurriedly moved away from the window, her pulses racing violently. He wasn't going to come in here, surely? He had only dropped Patti, she told herself, but all the same she listened tensely to the sound of footsteps and voices.

The knock on her door made her jump, she went to answer it reluctantly, her stomach churning at the prospect of facing Laird.

Patti seemed faintly nervous. 'Anna, Laird offered to come back later to drive us to the theatre—is that OK?' The words tumbled out too hastily and she was pink. It was obvious she was uncertain about Anna's reaction.

Anna looked at Laird distantly, her face masked. 'That's very kind of you,' she said without meaning it. Obviously he didn't like the idea of his sister travelling across London on a bus with her. That was OK for Anna; but unsuitable for Laird Montgomery's little sister. Did he also object to Patti being here at all?

His eyes were a flinty grey today, as hard as the rest of his face; she saw them slide past her and flick over the room.

'I'll be back at five-thirty,' he said crisply, then turned on his heel and vanished.

'You don't mind, do you?' Patti asked helplessly, and Anna made herself laugh and shake her head.

'Why should I mind driving in a Rolls instead of going on the bus?' She gestured. 'Come in and sit down; lunch is more or less ready. It's very simple, just soup and salad, I'm afraid.'

Patti sat down in the only chair, her eyes drifting around the room. Anna watched her face drily.

'Well, what do you think?'

'Golly!' said Patti on a stunned breath.

Anna laughed. 'Well, I told you living in digs was no fun, didn't I?'

'I didn't imagine anything like this, though,' Patti said naïvely, then looked back at Anna. 'I think you're terrific, Anna; putting up with this to do what you want to do! You could earn so much more as a secretary or something boring like that, then you wouldn't have to live in a place like this. I admire you, I don't know if I could do it.'

Anna watched her, a funny little smile curving her mouth. 'Well, if you couldn't, you don't want to be an actress that badly,' she said.

The other girl's face glowed suddenly. 'Oh, but I do,' she said. 'And if it meant living on what I earn at the moment, which is pathetic, anyway, I'd manage it somehow.' Then she grinned. 'I'm jolly glad I don't have to, all the same.'

As they ate lunch, they talked with more frankness than they had ever done before, and the time passed rapidly. Anna had a shock when she looked at her watch and saw it was gone five. Laird would be here soon, and she wasn't ready. Catching that glance, Patti looked at her own watch, exclaiming, 'Good heavens, is that the time?' She smiled across the room. 'It's been fun, Anna, I've enjoyed myself, and I've come to a decision—at the end of our run, I'm going to audition for drama school, and if I get a place I won't take up the chance to go with the rest of you into the West End, supposing that Joey offers me the chance, that is! My mother seems less hostile to the idea of me going on the stage, I think you talked her round—and she was surprised to see that I could act when she and Daddy came to the play. They'll let me go to drama school now, anyway, and I think it would be wiser to do that. I've loved being in a professional production, but I have such a tiny part and I think I've learnt everything I could from it, don't you?'

Anna smiled at her. 'I think you're making the right decision,' she agreed. Patti would never find out whether she could really act or not unless she spent some time training for the job; what she could pick up from being in a running play was not enough. She needed to study stage technique and voice production and a hundred other things.

Laird arrived exactly on time, and the two girls got into the back of the Rolls, driving off under intense scrutiny from the landlady's window.

'I see Mrs Gawton is still at her post,' Laird drawled, his eyes flicking back to meet Anna's.

'Your car gives her great status with the neighbours,' Anna said ruefully. 'She loves watching it drive up to her door.'

'But you don't?'

'*I'm* not a snob!' Anna bit out, not adding that every time she saw either him or his car she felt her nervous system go into overdrive. Patti gave her a puzzled, worried look and Anna relaxed deliberately; she must not snap at him like that in front of his sister, it would only make Patti even more curious.

He dropped them at the theatre and drove off with a cool farewell. Anna walked through the stage door, wishing she didn't feel so depressed and angry with herself because it was crazy to go on thinking about him, letting him dominate her mind in this way. She hadn't really stopped thinking about him since the morning they met, outside this theatre. That was just a few weeks ago; yet it seemed like years to her.

Joey called her to one side just before the curtain went up. 'I'd like to have a talk, Anna. Can we have lunch? How about Monday?'

'Of course, where?'

'I was thinking about that—remember the trattoria where I took the cast the day before we began rehearsing? That's very near your place, isn't it? Could we meet there? Around one o'clock?'

Anna nodded. 'I'll be there.' Why did Joey want to talk to her? she wondered uneasily, her heart sinking at the suspicion that he might be going to tell her that he wouldn't be taking her in the play when it transferred to the West End. Their run in the out-of-town little theatre was due to end in six weeks, but they still hadn't heard whether or not they would be transferring.

Anna had felt she was bound to keep her part; her reviews had all been good and Joey seemed pleased with her. She had had several press interviews since the play opened; it had been good publicity, spreading her name around.

Yet now she quaked with insecurity, her nerves in tatters, and she did not give a good performance that evening, which made her even more unhappy.

She walked to the restaurant, arriving in spring sunlight to find Joey waiting for her at the table. They ate melon and Parma ham followed by spaghetti, talking about the proposed move into the West End.

'We've been given a definite date now and a thea-tre—they're putting us into the Sheridan, which is exactly right for us, I think, don't you? Anything bigger would have swamped us. The only problem is the date—there's going to be a longer gap than I'd have liked. Two months.' He looked hard at Anna. 'I've spoken to Dame Floss and she's ready to sign it, how about you?'

She breathed with relief, laughing. 'Of course I will! I can always get a part-time job while I'm waiting.'

'Sure? I gathered you were pretty hard-up and I wouldn't want to lose you to someone else, we'd want you to sign the contract right away and we could give you an advance on your money.'

'That's good of you,' she said with surprise. 'I'll think about it and let you know, but as far as the play is concerned, I'll be happy to sign right away.'

As they left the restaurant Joey halted to buy a huge bunch of golden daffodils from a flower shop, thrusting them into Anna's arms with a smile.

'Thank you,' she said, taken aback but delighted, bending her head to inhale their faint perfume.

'Nice to see it really is spring,' he said humorously, glancing up at the pale blue sky. 'We may even get some summer if we wait long enough!'

He drove her back to her flat and pulled up outside to lean forward and eye the building with much the same wry distaste as Laird had shown. 'This is where you live? My God, Anna! I'll make sure you get that advance and when you've got it, find somewhere better than this to live!'

She laughed. 'Joey, if it meant I could go on acting, I'd be happy living in a dustbin!'

He considered her, his head to one side. 'I suppose it helps!'

'What?' she asked, bewildered.

'Being obsessed.' Joey leaned forward and kissed her lightly. 'As Dame Flossie keeps saying, it's a pleasure to work with you. I wish the rest of the company were as dedicated as you are.'

Anna met his eyes searchingly. 'Does that mean you aren't signing everyone?'

His mouth indented and he shook his head. 'Afraid not, no. Some people will be leaving us.'

'Who?'

'I can't tell you until I've told them, it wouldn't be fair, but I gather you already know that Patti will be one of them. Her choice, not mine, but I think she's sensible to start again at a good school. She's got a lot to learn. She should be very grateful to you for everything you've taught her.'

'Me?' Anna's eyes opened wide and Joey grinned at her.

'Yes, you, as if you didn't know. You've shown her what real dedication is and what it can cost to be an actress—if she's still determined to go on with the game, it's because she's seen how much you love it in spite of everything.'

She kissed him on the cheek. 'Don't be too nice, Joey. I'm not used to that from you and it makes me feel worried,' she teased, getting out of the car, her arms full of the vivid golden trumpets of the flowers he had given her. Joey drove off at once and Anna turned towards the gate. Out of the corner of her eye she caught a gleam of blue and silver and swung back again, staring in disbelief at the Rolls parked by the kerb some yards away. She hadn't even noticed it until then. Had it been there when she and Joey drove past? Or had it driven up behind them while they were talking in Joey's car?

Laird got out of it, pushing back a swathe of thick black hair as the wind whipped it over his face. Anna had a violent urge to run away, but she wouldn't give in to it. She stood her ground, holding the daffodils close to her like a barrier to keep him at a distance, frowning as he strolled towards her. His movements were casual, but his face was a threat.

She stared into his icy grey eyes without flinching, hiding her fear at what she read in them. 'What are you doing here?'

'Waiting for you,' he said tersely. 'That was Ross in the car, wasn't it? I didn't know you two were on kissing terms.'

Anna lifted her chin in defiance. 'Didn't you? Why were you waiting for me? I thought I'd made it clear that I didn't want to see you again.'

His eyes ran over her, halted on the flowers. 'Been wandering lonely as a cloud?'

'Joey gave them to me,' she said absently, then wished she hadn't admitted it, because Laird's face clenched in white fury.

'So that's why you turned me down? It was Ross all the time! Why not just say so? He isn't married, is he?'

'Joey had nothing to do with it,' snapped Anna, and began to walk towards the gate again.

Laird took two long strides and grabbed her arm. 'I've been waiting here for half an hour to talk to you, you're not walking out on me now. Come and sit in the car, I'm not going into that grim little cell you call a home.'

She began to pull herself free, her face dark red with anger. 'Don't you manhandle me!'

'Mrs Gawton's watching,' he taunted, and she glared up at him, biting her lip.

'I don't care if she is!'

'Liar! You've gone crimson. She scares the life out of you, and I don't mind admitting, she puts the fear of God into me. You must be tougher than you look if you can stay under the same roof as that lady without cracking.'

Anna felt him edging her towards the limousine and threw a quick look towards the house in time to see the lace curtain twitch. He wasn't lying; Mrs Gawton was there, at her usual watching post, eagerly observing everything, no doubt, and trying hard to hear what was being said, too. Sighing, she gave in and let Laird push her into the front passenger seat. He walked round and got in behind the wheel, but instead of turning to talk to her he started the engine.

'Here, what are you doing?' she asked, alarmed, sitting up in the seat.

'Taking you somewhere private, where we won't have an avid audience.'

'I've got to be at the theatre very soon!'

'I'll get you there.' He glanced down at the flowers she still held on her lap. 'You—and your precious daffodils!'

She had no chance of getting out of the car; it was already sweeping round the corner and heading westwards in a heavy stream of traffic. Anna looked at Laird's hard profile; her lashes quivering to hide her wary eyes. Where was he taking her? No prizes for guessing that, she told herself, and looked at the clock on the dashboard—it was a quarter to three and she had to be at the theatre by six-thirty at the very latest. It didn't take long to put on her make-up and costume, but she had to do other preparation, get herself into the part before she went on; and that meant spending a little time alone in the dressing-room before she was given her first call.

'Can't we talk in the car?' she said impatiently. 'If this is another of your attempts to persuade me to live with you, then . . . '

'It isn't,' he said shortly. 'I want to talk to you about Patti.'

'Oh.' That was a shock; she frowned ahead at the crowded road. 'What about Patti?'

'She told you she had applied for a place in this drama school?'

'She said she'd decided to, anyway.'

'Well, there's one small problem and I've come up with a possible solution, that's what I want to talk to you about.' He slowed and turned into the familiar underground car park, and Anna frantically searched her mind for some excuse for not going up to his penthouse again, but she could only think of one really cast-iron excuse to give—the truth.

Huskily, she gave that. 'I'm not going up there again,' she broke out. 'Whatever the reason! I don't want to remember what happened last time. You may not believe this, but I'd never . . . that was the first time I'd ever slept with anyone, and if I hadn't been drunk it wouldn't have happened. Just walking into that place would make me feel sick!'

Laird had switched off the engine and parked the car by the time her agitated voice broke off. He turned towards her, one arm over the wheel, his face calm and oddly almost ironic.

'I asked you once before how much you remembered,' he began, and Anna's face flooded with scalding colour.

'I remember waking up in your bed! I prefer to forget the rest.'

'What rest?' he enquired, and her eyes spat hatred at him.

'You know very well what I mean!'

'I'm not sure I do. What was it you particularly objected to—the fact that I carried you into the bedroom? Or that I undressed you and put you to bed? I can't see why you should feel so violently about either. You weren't too heavy for me! In fact, you're much too skinny and hardly weigh more than a child. And as for taking your clothes off—it was a pleasure, I assure you.'

Anna shook with temper. 'You really are a . . . '

'Bastard? Yes, you called me that before, and I still can't imagine why. I was the soul of chivalry, as soon as I'd gently stripped you I put you into the bed with no more than a cursory glance.'

She stared, beginning to sense that things weren't quite as straightforward as she had thought. His face was too amused; his eyes held nothing but a gentle mockery.

'When I woke up you were in bed with me,' she accused rather uncertainly.

'True.'

'Are you saying . . . you didn't . . . we didn't . . . ' She broke down in flushed confusion, and Laird smiled crookedly at her.

'Yes, I'm saying that—I didn't and we didn't. I spent most of the night on the couch, but I got a wry neck from sleeping on the damn thing because I'm just over six foot and the couch is five foot something. I got into bed with you at around three in the morning. You were snoring . . . '

'I was not!' she protested, laughing almost hysterically, tears in her eyes.

'No need to cry about it,' said Laird, producing a handkerchief and drying the tears with a gentle hand. 'I'm sorry to ruin your illusions, but you were distinctly snoring—the champagne, I've no doubt. You were dead to the world and I was as stiff as a board and freezing into the bargain—the bed looked warm and inviting.' He paused, his heavy-lidded eyes gleaming. 'So did you, of course, don't think I wasn't tempted, but I felt I needed a few hours' sleep more than anything else, so I climbed into bed and went out like a light. When I woke up, you'd gone.'

Anna shut her eyes, breathing roughly. 'Why didn't you tell me?'

'Tell you what, exactly?' he enquired drily. 'How was I to know that you had gone off with such romantic visions in your head? It certainly didn't occur to me to ring you up and say: by the way, I didn't seduce you the other night, in case you were wondering!'

Anna laughed angrily, then opened her eyes and gave him a glare. 'You knew later on, though! I as good as told you what I thought, and you didn't disillusion me.'

'I plead guilty,' he said, shrugging. 'You were giving me a bad time and I wasn't feeling very friendly towards you. I don't enjoy being shouted at by a woman. In fact, it makes my blood curdle, especially when I haven't done a thing to justify it, except try to make it plain that I find her attractive, and want to get to know her better.'

Anna bit her lip, looking down, and after a pause Laird went on drily, 'I came along to your flat to pick you up and take you to have lunch with my family, and walked into a barrage that nearly knocked me flat! By the time I'd caught on to what I was being accused of and realised what interesting assumptions you'd made, I was angry too, and childish enough to let you go on thinking whatever you liked!' He gave her a rueful, half-defiant grimace. 'Sorry!'

'You aren't sorry at all!' she accused, and he laughed impatiently.

'OK, I'm not. I think you asked for it—I behaved the way you apparently expected me to! People do, you know. Like dogs—if you scream every time you see a dog and run away, it will chase you and bite your leg. That's its nature.'

'Bite my leg and you'll be sorry!' muttered Anna, her green eyes feverish. 'I suppose it didn't occur to you that I might have had a bad time, too, thinking I'd slept with a total stranger?'

His face altered, a frown coming into it. 'Well, no,' he began slowly, and her temper leapt up.

'No, that was obvious! While you were busy resenting being shouted at, how do you think I felt? When I left here that morning I almost chucked myself in the river.'

'Oh, hell!' He moved closer and put out a hand to touch hers; Anna pushed it away furiously.

'Keep your damned hands to yourself! When I think . . . the hours of misery I went through . . . and all the time . . . My God, I could kill you!'

'How was I to know you were a virgin?' he asked, as if she wasn't being reasonable, and Anna's face was scarlet at once.

'Shut up!'

'It didn't occur to me until now, but if you knew anything about it you couldn't have suspected I'd made love to you—you weren't that drunk. I rather think you'd have woken up at some point in the proceedings.'

Anna felt like a boiled lobster. 'Will you stop talking about it?' she snarled at him, and Laird laughed softly.

'When I make love to you, Anna, you'll be fully conscious, I promise you,' he said, voice bland, 'and you'll know all about it.'

Confusion and rage combined to make Anna barely able to speak. She forced herself, nevertheless. She wasn't letting that past. 'If you think . . . I'd rather die . . . and stop grinning like a chimpanzee, I'll never let you . . . '

'Don't go incoherent on me again,' Laird urged. 'I have trouble enough interpreting what you're saying even when you're relatively coherent. When you start talking in bits and pieces you lose me entirely.'

Anna screwed up her hands and tried not to scream, but it wasn't easy. She couldn't stop thinking of all she had gone through and how easily he could have made the position clear. Instead, he had tormented and teased as if he was getting his own back about something. She looked at him scathingly.

'I'll tell you what I think . . . '

'Do,' he encouraged. 'I'd love to hear what you think. Frankly, at times I've begun to wonder if you can.'

'Oh . . . ' Anna seethed, shut her eyes, counted to ten, then went on doggedly, 'I think you have a grudge against women in general. You may have good reasons for being disenchanted with my sex, but that's no excuse for the way you've deliberately tormented me!'

'I've what? Aren't you overstating the case a little?' he interrupted impatiently.

'I don't think so. Asking me to move into your penthouse, offering me a luxury apartment with a jacuzzi—and it was all a tease!'

'You sound as if you're rather regretful about that!' he said, smiling.

'Oh, take me seriously!' Anna snapped.

His arched brows answered that and she took a long, rough breath before she went on, 'I'm sorry your marriage broke up, I'm sorry your wife was a bitch, and that your mother went away when you were small—I know it must have been very tough on you, all of that, but it had nothing to do with me, and I resent being made the scapegoat for what other women did to you before I even met you!'

Laird seemed to turn into a pillar of salt. He sat and stared at her fixedly, his face rigid and angular, his skin pale and his grey eyes glittering points of light between those heavy lids.

Anna swallowed, suddenly nervous. Maybe she shouldn't have said all that? Laird looked really alarming—he was furious, she could see that, and she looked away, disturbed by the fixity of his stare.

When he did speak, his voice had enough ice in it to sink the *Titanic*.

'You *have* had some fascinating chats, haven't you? With Patti, I suppose? Or my stepmother? Well, it doesn't matter which, but get one thing straight, Anna, I'm in no need of a psychiatrist, especially an amateur. My brains aren't scrambled and I wasn't working out my revenge on the whole female sex through you. I'm sorry I didn't immediately put you straight about what happened that night, but I was frankly insulted. What sort of guy do you think I am? Do I look as if I need to get a woman drunk before I can get her into bed? Or as if I'd enjoy making love to a woman who didn't even know what was going on?' He took a deep breath and swung away, opened the door and got out of the Rolls.

Anna almost fell out of the car when he loomed up at her side of it. He took the daffodils she was still clutching and tossed them in a cavalier fashion into the back seat. 'You can pick them up when I drive you to the theatre,' he said brusquely as he marched her to the lift.

Both of them were silent as they soared up to the top floor of the building. Anna didn't know whether she was more relieved or furious; her mind was in utter chaos.

Parsons opened the door, scowling. 'You, is it?' He stood back to let them enter, peered at Anna and gave an eldritch cackle. 'Hallo, miss, 'ow are you? Come for dinner? I've got a nice bit of steak 'andy, in case you come agin.'

'No, we haven't come for dinner,' Laird told him. 'Get back to your lair, I'll look after the lady.'

'I'll bet,' said Parsons, slouching off, muttering to himself as he shut the door.

Laird moved to the cocktail cabinet and asked, 'Can I get you a drink?'

'No, you certainly cannot!' Anna said vehemently, and he laughed.

'No, maybe not. How about a glass of pineapple juice or tomato juice?'

'Tomato juice would be nice, thanks. What was it you wanted to talk about? Patti, you said?'

He brought her the glass of tomato juice and waved her to a chair while he flung himself down on the couch, holding a glass of whisky.

'There's a problem about Patti going to drama school,' he began. 'Her parents have just decided to sell the house in Wolfstone Square and live permanently in the country. They've had a cottage in Sussex for years, they'll live there full time now, but Patti couldn't commute from there, so she needs somewhere to live in London. She could move in here with me, in fact, I first of all suggested that, but I'm sometimes away for a week or two at a time and she'd be alone here, so her mother wasn't very happy with that idea.' He drank some of his whisky, watching Anna. 'And that's where you come in. How would you feel about sharing a flat with Patti?'

CHAPTER EIGHT

ANNA was taken aback by the suggestion; she stared at him incredulously, her green eyes enormous and her lips parting in an audible intake of air.

Laird smiled wryly. 'And before you jump to any more of your wild conclusions, I am not suggesting that I should pay your rent, nor would I be moving in with you.'

She ignored that, concentrating on the practical side of the idea. 'I can only just afford the rent I'm paying now,' she pointed out. 'I'm sure Patti would want somewhere a lot better than the place I've got.'

'You can bet on it,' he agreed.

'And I couldn't put up half the rent for the sort of flat she would want!'

'There wouldn't be any rent,' Laird said smoothly, and her face tightened suspiciously. 'No need to glare like that,' he went on. 'This isn't my idea, it came from Patti's mother in the beginning. We've just finished a new block of flats down near the river, close to the Tower of London. We haven't sold them all yet; a number are still vacant and it occurred to my stepmother that Patti might like one of them. They're quite central, only fifteen minutes from the West End and the theatres, but Patti's still very young and she's never lived alone, so it seemed much better for her to share the flat. Of course, we could advertise for someone who would pay rent, but that would be risky. You never know who you're getting, and if

Patti took a dislike to them after they'd moved in, it might be hard to get them out again.'

Anna nodded soberly. 'I thought of sharing a flat myself, at one time, but apart from not being able to afford much rent I didn't like any of the people I'd have had to live with.'

'Exactly. That's why we thought of you. Patti knows you, you've obviously become friends and my parents liked you when they met you. You'd be doing them a big favour if you accepted their offer. Patti wouldn't be paying any rent, of course—the flat will be in her name, legally she will be the owner as my father is giving it to her, and we wouldn't want any rent from you, either.'

Anna hesitated, frowning. 'Your mother never mentioned it to me when I had lunch at the house.'

'She wanted to talk it over with my father and Patti first. The offer for the house had only just been made; they hadn't quite decided what to do that weekend, but my father finds living in central London very tiring; he's an old man and he wants to end his days in the peace and quiet of the countryside. He's been spending half the year in Sussex anyway, with his roses and his bee-keeping, but they were reluctant to sell the old house. Dad has lived there since he was first married, forty years ago. That's a long time. But the house is far too big for a small family and Dad doesn't entertain as much as he used to.

'It's enormous,' Anna agreed. 'I did wonder about that when I was there. With just the three of them, and all those rooms.'

'It's ridiculous,' said Laird, grimacing. 'Anyway, they've definitely decided to sell and they plan to leave for Sussex in six weeks. It will take that long to arrange for their furniture to be sold and the rest of the things they'll be keeping taken down to the cottage. That's why they want your answer so quickly. They want to get Patti settled as soon as possible.'

Anna put down her half-finished tomato juice and frowned around the room while she thought about it.

'Well?' Laird prompted as she glanced back at him.

'Before I decide, I'd like to talk to Patti about it. After all, it's Patti who'll have to live with me—I want to be quite sure she likes the idea.'

'That's reasonable, I suppose,' he said reluctantly. 'If I do move into this flat, how soon would . . . '

'Next month some time? Before the move to Sussex, obviously.'

'I'd have to give notice to Mrs Gawton.' Anna's eyes began to gleam and her mouth curved upward in a gleeful smile, and Laird laughed softly, watching her.

'I see you can't wait.'

'No, it will be a pleasure,' Anna admitted, laughing, then said rather defiantly, 'But about rent . . . I would feel awkward not paying any, it would put me in an invidious position, you must see that. When we start our West End run I would be able to pay a fair rent, and that's what I'd like to do.'

Laird gave a little shrug. 'If you insist.'

'I do.'

'Then I won't waste my time trying to talk you out of it,' he said, getting to his feet. 'Now, I'd better drive you to the theatre, or are you going to finish that tomato juice?'

She loooked at the glass, her eyes rueful. 'I'm sorry, would you mind if I don't?'

'Why should I?' he asked calmly, moving to the door. 'Let's go, then. I still have a lot of work to do today.'

Parsons peered out from another door as they left. 'You off, then?'

'What does it look like?' Laird asked him over his shoulder.

'Can't even ask a civil question without getting my head bit off,' the old man snarled, as they walked into the corridor.

'I'll be in late, leave me some sandwiches,' Laird directed, shutting the front door, but Parsons had the last word, he yelled through it loudly enough for them to hear him from the other end of the building.

'Nothing to put in 'em!'

Laird pressed the lift button unconcernedly. As they descended a moment later, Anna asked him, 'This lift doesn't stop at any other floors, does it?'

'It can do, if you want it to—I do work here, you know. I have a large office on the floor below the penthouse and I'm usually at my desk by half past eight each morning. I use the stairs more than I use the lift, coming and going to my office, I mean. If I'm going to another floor in the building, I use the lift.'

'But there's never anybody else in this lift. The place is like a ghost town.'

Laird surveyed her with wry amusement. 'My dear girl, this is *my* lift. There are a whole battery of lifts for the staff, but they're in the front of the building.'

'You have a lift all to yourself?' Anna's eyes opened wide.

'You sound quite shocked.'

'It seems very extravagant. How do the staff get from the car park to their offices?' she asked as they walked from the lift to the Rolls. Her eyes skimmed the rows of other cars parked in the dimly lit vault whose concrete ceiling made her voice and footsteps echo back to her.

'They use the lifts at the other end.' Laird unlocked the Rolls and opened the door for her.

'While you sail upstairs in lonely splendour?' she jeered.

'Get in the car, you little wasp,' Laird told her impatiently.

As they were driving to the theatre, Anna asked, 'Why was it you who put this idea up to me? Why not Patti?'

'She was afraid you'd turn the idea down, she preferred me to suggest it to you—a disinterested third party!'

She gave him a sidelong glance of irony and he met it with a bland smile.

'You mean, you insisted on doing it?' she derided, and he laughed.

'I'm a great believer in economy of effort.'

'Very gnomic, but what does it mean?'

'It means that it killed two birds with one stone for me to talk to you about Patti—I was able to put the case to you without embarrassing you, and if either Patti or her mother had suggested it you might have found it awkward to refuse!' He paused as he took a corner and Anna urged impatiently, 'And?'

Laird's eyes mocked her as he looked round at her. 'And it gave me a chance to get you up to my penthouse,' he teased in a deep, big-bad-wolf voice.

'Oh, shut up!' she said crossly, but couldn't help laughing. He drew up outside the theatre and she knew that she did not want to get out of the Rolls and walk away from him, she sat there for a moment, looking at him with a smile while Laird looked back at her, his grey eyes full of warmth.

'Thank you for the lift,' Anna said huskily, and he leaned towards her as if he was going to kiss her. At once she felt an upsurge of panic and turned away, fumbling with the door. She scrambled out on to the pavement and shut the door again; as soon as she had the Rolls shot away with a muted roar, and Anna walked into the theatre, biting her lip. Why had she felt like that? Laird had been angry at her silent rejection; she had caught one glimpse of his face and had been frightened by the rigidity of it.

Why am I feeling guilty? she asked herself, suddenly furious. Why should I feel I ought to apologise, just because I didn't want him to kiss me? Why should I let him kiss me if I don't want it?

She walked into the dressing-room, scowling, and in the mirror met Patti's eyes.

'Is something wrong?'

Anna pulled herself together, dismissing Laird from her head. 'No, sorry, I was thinking about something . . .'

She dropped into the chair next to Patti and propped her head on her hands, staring into the mirror. Every time she saw herself she felt the same twinge of unfamiliarity—somehow, somewhere, she had altered, she wasn't the same girl she had been a few months ago. Being in this play had changed her, of course; she knew she had discovered something about herself and about other people simply from working with Joey and Dame Flossie and the others. It was more than that, though; the alteration ran deep inside her.

'Have you talked to Laird?' Patti asked uncertainly, and Anna's eyes flicked sideways to meet the other girl's mirrored ones.

'Yes,' she nodded, smiling.

'Will you share the flat with me?' Eagerness showed in Patti's eyes, deepening their blue. 'It would be terrific fun, Anna. I've never lived away from home, except at school, and that doesn't really count, does it? You're still treated as a child and you don't have any freedom.' She had her chin cupped on her hand and was smiling excitedly. 'I can't believe my mother's going to let me!'

Anna watched her ruefully; how could she refuse when Patti was so lit up with happiness? 'Let's discuss it before we make up our minds what to do,' she said warily, but she knew very well that she was going to move into that flat, in spite of the prickling of her pride. She would pay as much as she could towards the rent, she assured herself. She wouldn't let the Montgomery family take her over—she wasn't a charity case!

'There are one or two conditions on my side,' she said, and Patti nodded, listening intently.

'Oh, of course, I understand how you feel, and Laird didn't mean to hurt your feelings, none of us did,' Patti stammered when she had finished. 'You suggest the rent you want to pay and . . . didn't you talk about it? I thought Laird would fix all that, I didn't know what to say, I . . . '

Flushed and unhappy, she broke down, and Anna sighed. 'OK, I'll fix it with Laird.'

Patti was still worried. 'But you do want to share the flat, don't you?' she asked, and Anna laughed, shedding her own pride, trying to make Patti smile again.

'You've seen where I'm living now! What do you think?'

Patti giggled, relaxing. 'No more Mrs Gawton!'

'No more spiders in the bath . . . '

'Ugh, are there really?'

'Every time you look!' Anna assured her. 'No more freezing water or draughts or sharing a bathroom with four other people.' She looked at her watch and groaned. 'Oh, no! Look at the time—I'm nowhere near ready yet. Don't talk to me any more, Patti, let me get my make-up on!'

Laird took them to see the flat a few days later. It was on the corner of the block, on the third floor, just high enough to give them a view of the Thames but removing them from the bustle and noise of the waterfront below. There were two small bedrooms, a rectangular sitting-room, a modern, fully fitted kitchen and a bathroom which Anna gazed at with delight, the tiles a lemony shade and the fittings a darker yellow. What made Anna's eyes glisten was the shower cubicle, with frosted glass door and gleaming chrome fittings.

'No more spiders!' Patti teased.

'Spiders?' enquired Laird, looking from one to the other.

'A private joke,' Anna told him.

'Come and stand on the balcony, Anna,' Patti urged, running across the corridor into the sitting-room. Anna followed her out on to the balcony and they leaned on the iron rail to stare out across the busy river and the skyline beyond. The morning was warm, the sky blue, the vista breathtaking.

'We'll be able to sunbathe out here!' Patti swung to measure the width of the balcony with two hands. 'We can easily get a couple of loungers into this space, and a little table, to put our iced drinks on!'

'I foresee orgies,' drawled Laird, and his half-sister giggled.

'We might even invite you to dinner!'

His brows rose. 'Who'll be doing the cooking? Not you, I hope?'

Patti made a face at him. 'I'll learn, by trial and error!'

'Not on me, you won't!' He turned back into the sitting-room, his footsteps echoing on the bare floor. 'Now, about furnishing the place—do you want to pick stuff from home? It will mostly be sold if you don't.'

Patti gave Anna an enquiring look. 'What do you think?'

'It seems sensible. Why buy new furniture when you can get it without buying it?'

'If we go back to Wolfstone Square for lunch, you can go round with your mother afterwards and pick out what you want,' Laird suggested.

'What do you think, Anna?' Patti asked again, looking at her for a lead. 'Will you come and help me pick out what we need? You'll have a better idea than me.'

'We won't want too much furniture,' said Anna, running an eye over the rooms and realising that they were none of them particularly large. 'I like lots of space and light.'

'Oh, me too,' Patti agreed eagerly.

They walked around the flat together, noting down the essentials such as beds and chairs and chest of drawers for each of them, and ten minutes later drove away from the flat talking cheerfully. Anna felt rather disorientated; she had fallen from the real, everyday world of Mrs Gawton and spiders in the bath and baked beans on toast for lunch into a dizzying new world where none of the rules she had learnt applied. Patti had no idea about money or necessity. She had always been given what she asked for and hadn't had to worry or plan or budget.

Anna found it disturbing—one minute she was at ease with Laird and Patti; the next she came up against the fact that they couldn't understand her, or the background she came from—any more than she could understand them. Wasn't it crazy to get even more involved with them? Anna's common sense was as strong as her pride; she could already see the problems ahead when she moved into the flat with Patti. It began and ended with money, of course, and extended to everything; because Patti's upbringing and awareness of that glittering security net her family money gave her, had formed her attitudes, from the clothes she wore to whether she took a taxi instead of a bus. It was the tiny, fundamental things that made or wrecked a friendship. Anna was very uneasy as she followed Laird and Patti into their family home.

Naomi Montgomery was openly delighted because Anna would be sharing the flat with Patti. 'I shall sleep easy at night knowing she's with someone I can trust,' she said. 'If she insists on doing this drama course, at least I'll be sure of that!'

'You make Anna sound like a nanny,' Patti muttered irritably, grimacing at her mother.

Hugh Montgomery chuckled. 'I never had a nanny that looked like that, worse luck! Don't I wish I had?'

Laird shook his head reprovingly at his father. 'Tut, tut! I'm ashamed of you, Dad. At your age, too!'

'What's my age got to do with anything? You're never too old to admire a beautiful woman.'

Laird glanced at Anna through his lashes, his mouth wicked. 'There's hope for me yet, then. Some days when I get up I feel very old indeed.

'You ought to get married again,' Hugh Montgomery told him with cheerful frankness, and Laird stopped smiling.

'Oh, no! Once bitten, twice shy. I'll never get married again.'

CHAPTER NINE

IT WAS, in fact, a month before they moved into the new flat, and during that time Anna saw a great deal of Laird. She had lunch with his family several times; Laird picked her up and took her home or to the theatre. Sometimes Patti came, too; sometimes she didn't.

It surprised and disturbed Anna that she and Laird found so much to talk about. Talk between them was too easy; she did not want to enjoy being with him that much. They shared too many interests: poetry, the theatre, books, art, music . . . they had no sooner started discussion on one subject than the talk flowed into another and then another. She was finding out what sort of man Laird was, and yet she sensed that for all their rapport and casual chat, there was a distance between them. Laird's charm and warmth hid a core of his personality she couldn't guess at, and, she felt, would never reach because he barred the way.

One Saturday evening he was in the audience, sitting in the front row, and once Anna had spotted him she found her performance unaccountably going to pieces. Her symptoms were those of acute shock: heart going wild, breathing too rapid, colour first red, then white. She stumbled over her lines and Dame Flossie gave her a worried look, delivering her own words with her customary perfection.

Anna tried to pull herself together, only to dry. Mouth full of ashes, she stared at Dame Flossie imploringly and got a mouthed cue, Dame Flossie's head turned away from the audience so that they should not see her lips move.

Anna thankfully delivered her line and kept her eyes away from the front row where Laird's face glimmered in the darkness. After that she managed to stay in the part, evicting him from her consciousness.

In her dressing-room she looked at Joey and Dame Flossie with humble apology. 'Sorry, it won't happen again.'

'My dear, it happens to us all,' Dame Flossie said with her usual generosity, but Joey was not so sympathetic.

'What exactly did happen? It isn't like you—something on your mind? If you've got a problem and I can help . . . '

'No, there are no problems, thanks, Joey.'

His brow darkened. 'Then for God's sake keep your mind on the bloody play!'

When he had slammed out, Dame Flossie shook her head. 'Joey's temper is fraying at the edges! He's working too hard; he's just started rehearsing a new play at the National, trying to cut himself in half, doesn't work, doesn't work.'

She patted Anna's cheek as Anna stammered, 'Sorry I lost my place like that, I'm glad it didn't throw you.'

'Throw me?' An incredulous amusement showed in the old face. 'Never in this life, my dear.' She went back to her own dressing-room, and Patti and Anna grinned at each other.

'Laird's out front,' Patti said.

'I know.' Anna kept her eyes on her reflection as she ran a comb through her hair. She did not want Patti to guess why she had dried like that. Most of all, she did not want Laird to guess.

'He didn't tell me he was coming,' Patti murmured, putting on her coat.

Anna was taking a long time to change and remove her make-up. She said with careful offhandedness, 'Don't wait for me, off you go!'

'That's OK—we'll give you a lift home,' Patti said innocently, lingering. Anna could have screamed; she didn't dare admit that the last thing she wanted was to see Laird. She still hadn't recovered from the blinding shock of suddenly seeing him when she wasn't expecting to; that moment had cut the ground from under her feet and shown her how deeply she was in love.

When the two girls left the stage door Laird was there, leaning against his Rolls, his arms crossed and his lean body casually graceful. Anna had herself under command now, though.

'Where's the top hat and opera cloak?' she mocked, and his brows rose.

'What?'

'Wasn't that what stage door Johnnies wore?'

He eyed her drily, opening the passenger door of the Rolls. 'Get in, dear Lady Disdain.' Laughing, Anna obeyed.

Patti looked blankly at him. 'What?' She slid in beside Anna and Laird walked round to get behind the wheel. 'What did he call you?' Patti asked Anna, and as he got into the driver's seat Laird glanced round, his mouth crooked.

'It's a quotation from *Much Ado about Nothing*,' Anna told Patti, looking into Laird's smiling eyes.

'Oh, Shakespeare,' said Patti, shrugging the poet away. 'I've never wanted to act in Shakespeare. Have you, Anna?'

'I did some while I was in rep.'

'Don't tell me,' Laird teased. 'You were a fairy in *A Midsummer Night's Dream?*'

'Actually, I played Iras in *Antony and Cleopatra*, and don't be so sarcastic.' She glanced out of the window, frowning. 'Where are you taking us?'

'To supper, I booked a table for three at a Greek restaurant. You'll love the food, they're authentic, and it's small, we won't find ourselves in a crowd.' He threw a glance over his shoulder at her. 'Sunday tomorrow, you don't have to work; so going to bed a little later than usual won't hurt.'

'I'm rather tired,' said Anna, afraid of spending too much time with him; that would only feed her addiction to him, make it harder for her to deal with the way she felt.

'You need to unwind,' he coolly decided for her. 'After a performance you're always on a high. What you need is a little company and good food.'

'Don't tell me what I need!' she muttered. 'What would you know about it, anyway? Have you ever put a foot on a stage?'

'I've heard Joey Ross talking about it,' Laird informed her firmly. 'Stop arguing, woman, and let yourself be spoiled.'

Patti looked from one to the other, her expression worried. 'Don't you like Greek food, Anna?'

Anna gave in, sighing. 'I love it, I just thought I ought to get some sleep, that's all.'

'You can sleep tomorrow as late as you like,' Laird told her in his high-handed way, and she gave him a sideways look of extreme irritation.

'Yes, sir, of course, sir,' she said, but made no impression on that thick hide. He just grinned in amusement as he pulled up outside the restaurant.

'That's better,' he said with satisfaction.

'I thought you'd like it.' If Anna hoped to wipe the smug grin off his face she was disappointed. Her sarcasm only made him laugh.

'All work and no play, Anna, will make you more and more tired and in the end it will wreck your acting. You have to take time off occasionally, relax and enjoy yourself, put back in what you've been giving out night after night.'

Patti nodded vigorously, her eyes on Anna's face, and Anna gave a wry smile as she followed them into the Greek restaurant. She regretted quarrelling with Laird in front of Patti; it had upset his half-sister, and Anna didn't want to worry Patti. The girl was surprisingly sensitive to atmosphere and shrank from loud voices and frowns, perhaps because she had seen so little of either in her own home. Patti's parents were calm and peaceful people, especially her mother. Naomi Montgomery might be years younger than her husband, but she had such a warm and gentle personality that when you were with them both you forgot the large age gap between them. Brought up in that cloudless household, Patti was unused to the rough and tumble of noisy discussion and argument.

Laird was right about the food in the Greek restaurant; it was particularly good and Anna enjoyed it more than she had expected. She had vine leaves stuffed with a mixture of rice and vegetables, followed by souvlakia, a lamb dish she had never tried before but which seemed rather less indigestible than the alternative—a dish of squid with rice which she was sure would give her nightmares at this time of the evening. Laird had the squid and, noticing the fascinated repulsion with which she stared at his plate, asked teasingly if she would like to try some.

'No, thanks,' said Anna, shuddering. 'It looks as if it might slither off the plate any minute and come and get me!'

'What a dramatic life you lead,' Laird mocked, eyeing her through his lashes. 'Such narrow escapes from all these threats which seem to surround you! If it isn't men trying to grab you, it's monsters from the deep.' He slid a fork under a squid tentacle and waved it at her.

Patti giggled. Anna bared her teeth at him. 'Very funny,' she said her face flushed, her heart thumping behind her breastbone in a distinctly nervy way. Did he have to make that pointed comment when Patti was sitting there listening? Anna hated to remember the stupid conclusions she had jumped to—he must think she was very naïve and unsophisticated, a wide-eyed innocent. That was how she had seen Patti—she hadn't dreamt it could apply to herself, it was horribly embarrassing to admit what a fool she had been, but she hadn't any experience to compare it with, had she? If she had ever been to bed with a man she would have known, presumably.

Her brow wrinkled. But how? she wondered, getting even more pink. She had an intensely vivid memory of how she had felt next day; she had been so sure that while she was too drunk to remember it Laird had made love to her. It had all been in her own mind, though. She believed Laird, and yet her unconscious had conjured up such powerful images of them making love that it was hard to admit it had all been her own imagination.

Did I dream them? she wondered, her pulses beating wildly at wrist and throat. Is that what happened? That night I dreamt about him, dreamt he made love to me, and woke up convinced it had really happened because there he was in bed next to me, just as he had been in the dream? The human mind led a life of its own, Joey Ross had said to the cast only that morning in rehearsal. If her mind was leading a secret life, Anna blushed to imagine what it got up to, and she was very glad Laird could not see inside her head. Those cool, intelligent eyes didn't have X-ray vision. Or did they? she thought as she met them across the table and saw the smile glimmering in them.

'What's funny?' she asked suspiciously.

'You have such an expressive face,' he drawled. 'I've been trying to work out what you've been thinking—you've scowled and grimaced in the most extraordinary way. Let us in on the secret.'

'You wouldn't like it if I told you,' Anna said, tossing back her cloudy red hair in defiance. She had no intention of giving away anything more to him—Laird already had far too much knowledge of the way her mind worked. That made her very uneasy.

Deliberately changing the subject, she asked him, 'What will happen to the rocking horse when the contents of the house are sold?'

He smiled at her, his hard face relaxed and almost tender. 'Worried about it? Were you thinking of putting in a bid?'

'I suppose it would be expensive?'

'Oh, it should go for quite a high figure,' Laird agreed. 'It's Victorian and very sought-after. Toys can be collectors' items these days.' His eyes held a gentle amusement. 'But it won't be up for auction with the rest of the furniture—I'm keeping it, for old times' sake. I've already had a few things transferred to the penthouse, the ones I can't bear to part with.'

Anna watched him intently. 'I thought you said the toys in the nursery were for Patti's children?'

'What?' asked Patti, sitting up and laughing. 'Give me a chance! It will be years before I think about having any kids.

'Exactly,' Laird drawled. 'And in the meantime, I'll give a home to my favourites from the nursery.'

'He had a whole vanload of stuff taken to his place,' Patti told Anna. 'Teddy bears and tin soldiers . . . '

'I thought you weren't sentimental,' Anna teased, and he gave her a sardonic glance.

'They're an investment, as I said—toys are valuable antiques when they're that old.' He gestured to her coffee. 'Are you going to drink that? We ought to be leaving soon, it's getting late.' His manner made it clear that the subject was closed. Laird was not going to admit to any sentimental fondness for such childish things as rocking horses and teddy bears. That might spoil his self-image; ruin his reputation for being a tough, hard-headed businessman.

Anna's green eyes mocked him, but she said nothing more. She was glad to hear that the rocking horse he called Dandy had not been scheduled for auction.

When Laird dropped her at her flat he murmured, 'Enjoyed yourself after all? I told you you would, didn't I?'

'And you're always right, of course,' Anna jeered, fleeing before he could answer, but the trouble was, she thought as she tried to get to sleep that night, she *had* enjoyed herself! Far too much! The more she saw of Laird the harder she found it to expel his image from her heart. He threatened her peace of mind.

'I've got to do something about that man!' she told herself sternly, turning over restlessly in an attempt to settle down to sleep.

She slept late next morning and woke to find the room full of bright sunlight and the sound of birds. Drowsily, she leaned on her windowsill and watched a man in the street cleaning his car, some children playing on bikes, two women talking on their doorsteps. Sunday morning was always quiet in this street because so many of the residents worked hard all week and preferred to sleep late on a Sunday.

With reluctance, Anna went to have a bath and get dressed, then put on a jacket and went for a walk in the local park to feed the squirrels, buying a bag of peanuts from a vendor at the gate who overcharged her, of course.

'How much?' she asked, incredulous, and he shrugged.

'Take it or leave it, love. Plenty of customers around!' As she threw nuts to a bushy-tailed grey squirrel a few minutes later, Anna was forced to realise how right he was. The spring sunshine had brought dozens of people out to the park with the same idea as herself. All the paths between the trees were crowded with people hoping to entice the squirrels, taking snapshots of them as they scurried up and down trees and paused to sit up, their tiny paws gripping a nut while they neatly nibbled away at it. Anna had never been allowed to have a pet and had always yearned to have one. She might resent being grossly overcharged by the peanut vendor, but it gave her quite a kick to watch the bright-eyed little creatures so close to her and she was angry when three teenage boys ran up, shouting, deliberately frightening the squirrels back up their trees.

'Why did you do that?' she snapped, turning on the boys, who jeered at her. One reached out and grabbed the bag of nuts she held and ran off with it. Flushed and furious, Anna pursued him and his friends along the leafy path and through the formal flower garden by the lake. They darted out of the elaborate iron-work gates and Anna followed, gradually gaining on them, although she wasn't sure what she would do if she caught up. It made her even angrier to find herself crunching over nut shells and to know that as they ran the boys were eating her peanuts. They kept looking back and grinning as they chucked peanut shells down, without slackening their pace.

She finally came within touching distance of them and with a furious leap grabbed one by his jacket. He turned and hit out at her, kicking her at the same time, and his friends halted and ran back to launch an attack too.

Anna could have coped with one of them, but all three were too much for her. She was so busy fending them off that she didn't notice the blue and silver Rolls or hear the screech of the tyres as the driver jammed on his brakes. The first she knew of Laird's arrival was when two of her attackers fled. She was still holding the third by his jacket, her face pink with anger and exertion, her green eyes spitting fury.

Laird removed him and gripped him by the shoulder in a punishing hold which made the boy wriggle sullenly. However, he summed Laird up in one lightning glance that absorbed his height and muscle and decided a struggle would be useless and very probably unpleasant.

'What the hell's going on?' Laird demanded as Anna blinked at him in surprise.

'I was feeding the squirrels in the park and they ran up and scared them off, and then they stole my bag of peanuts and they . . .

'I didn't do nothing!' the boy yelled. 'Leggo, you big brute . . . '

'Ate them all,' Anna ended, her eyes following the betraying trail of peanut shells leading back to the park gates.

'I'll tell my mum,' the boy threatened, twisting in Laird's grasp.

'It's against the law to drop litter in a public place,' Laird said. 'Now, you'll pick up everyone of those nutshells and drop them into the litter bin at the park gates.'

'Like hell!' the boy sneered, darting forward, but the strong hand clenched on his shoulder again and he winced. 'Who d'you think you are?'

'Come on,' said Laird, propelling him towards the nearest scattering of shells. Anna stood and watched as the boy reluctantly picked up the shells until he reached the park gates where Laird watched him shed them all into the litter bin. The boy was then marched back to Anna.

'Tell the lady you're sorry,' ordered Laird.

'Sorry, lady,' the boy muttered sulkily.

'Graciously said,' Laird told him with sarcasm. 'Now, clear off, and in future behave yourself in the park. What's funny about ruining other people's enjoyment? Can't you find something better to do?'

'Like what?' sneered the boy. 'And anyway, we was only having a bit of fun—she didn't want those nuts, she was feeding them to the squirrels anyway, why'd she chase after us and make all that fuss?'

Laird had let go of him; he began to run, turning once to make a very rude gesture towards them before pelting off at top speed.

Laird looked drily at Anna. 'He has a point—why did you chase after them?'

'I was annoyed!'

He considered her, lifting one hand to brush down some of her windblown, cloudy red hair. 'You're crazy, you know that? When I saw you running after those boys, I thought you looked no older than they were—when are you going to grow up? You're a female Peter Pan.'

She knew she must look very dishevelled in her old blue jeans and green sweater, with shabby track shoes on her feet, but she still bristled. 'What are you doing in this neighbourhood, anyway?'

'I was bored, so I came to see you,' Laird said pleasantly, and she glared at him.

'Oh, thanks! I've got better things to do than amuse you whenever you're bored! And I'm not dressed for visiting your home, anyway, so if you're here to invite me to lunch . . . '

'I'm not. We're going on a picnic,' he said, taking her by the arm and relentlessly inserting her into the front of the Rolls in spite of her efforts to escape. He clipped the safety belt around her, saying, 'And stay there!' as he shut the door. Anna didn't have time to free herself before he was behind the wheel and the smooth purr of the engine started a second later.

'It can't be much fun for those boys, living around here,' Laird thought aloud as he drove off. 'Any more than it is for you. Is that how you usually spend your Sundays? Walking in the park, feeding the squirrels?'

'Sometimes I take a bus to the Tate Gallery or the National Gallery. I like looking at the pictures, and it's free. There are lots of free things to do in London on a Sunday—if the weather's fine,' Anna said soberly, then added, 'Take me home, I'm not going on a picnic with you! I've got other plans.'

'And Parsons went to so much trouble, too! After I'd told him who the picnic was for, that is—you've made a conquest there. I never knew the old man had such a soft spot for green eyes.' Laird gave her a glinting sideways smile.

Anna was touched but said defiantly, 'I like him.'

'I promised to tell him how you enjoyed the food,' Laird murmured seductively.

She bit her lip; tempted but still cautious. 'He's a marvellous cook—you're very lucky, I hope you know that.'

'It doesn't do to tell him so too often; he gets complacent and then he starts drinking. I have to keep him on a very tight rein.' Laird was heading eastwards, which puzzled her. Where was he taking her? 'He packed a hamper full of cold chicken, salads, home-made game chips . . . '

'What?' Anna asked, baffled.

'Crisps, to you,' Laird said with a grin. 'And some champagne in a vacuum ice-bucket, but that was my contribution.'

Anna felt a wave of hot colour sweeping up to her hairline; Laird saw it and gave her a quick, frowning look.

'That wasn't a taunt!'

'Wasn't it?' She turned and looked out of the window. 'Will you take me home, please?' Last time she had drunk champagne alone with him she had ended up in his bed, whether or not Laird had taken advantage of the fact. She had no intention of repeating that mistake.

'On a lovely day like this you ought to get out of London,' he informed her coolly. 'I'm taking you to the forest.'

'What forest?' she asked, taken aback by that.

'Epping, of course. Where do you think we're heading?'

'I've never been there,' she admitted, and he turned a look of incredulous amusement to her.

'Then you should have been! Don't you know what a long, hard fight Londoners had to stop property developers from building all over it, more than a century ago? And it's right on your doorstep—get on the bus or the underground, and you're there in half an hour, out of those dirty little streets where you live and into the open forest. And it's as free as a trip to the Tate, Anna.'

She gave him a surprised, dry look. 'Aren't *you* a property developer?' she asked scornfully.

'That's why I'm interested in the forest,' Laird told her calmly. 'Do you think I want to see every spare inch of ground covered in bricks and mortar? The quality of life's as important as a roof over the head for people who are homeless, Anna. One of the things my firm pride themselves on is landscaping gardens around the estates we build. I make sure we plant plenty of trees, in the roads and in the gardens. If there are established trees on the site when we move on to it, we keep as many as we can—nothing adds to an estate like trees.'

She was so interested in that discussion that she stopped asking to be taken home, which was possibly Laird's intention, she decided as she realised they were slowing to turn into an open clearing at the edge of the forest, set aside as a car park and already half full of cars. Laird walked round to the boot of the car and got out a wicker hamper and a tartan rug. Anna began to wander away, staring into the ranks of tall beech and oak rooted among earthy-scented waves of green fern. Sunlight filtered down through new and intensely vivid leaves, shadows flickered on the paths. Somewhere she heard children's voices, laughter; somewhere she heard the thud of hooves on a sandy bridle path, yet she could see nothing but trees and grass and windblown fern. The forest looked empty; the people from the cars parked in the car park had been swallowed up among the trees.

They walked along the wide track for a few moments, then Laird took a fork towards the left and followed a narrow path between clutching brambles and ferns which eventually opened out into a forest clearing, a small circle of leaf-littered grass between a ring of trees.

Spreading the tartan rug on the grass, he flung himself down on his back, his hands linked as a pillow for his head, and gazed up at the patch of blue sky above where the leafy branches did not quite meet. 'Spring's my favourite time of year,' he said with a little sigh of contentment. 'It's gentle and hopeful; it always makes you feel optimistic.'

Anna knelt down on the edge of the rug and opened the hamper to gloat over the contents. Laird watched her through half-closed lids, his mouth crooked with amusement.

'Why do I always get the feeling you're half starved? You're like one of those stray kittens you see in Rome—all ribs and great, hungry eyes, but when you bend down to stroke it, it spits and humps its back and claws you.'

'I may claw you, I may even spit, but I won't hump my back,' Anna said. 'Shall I unpack the food?'

'In a minute. Lie down and just drink in the silence,' he commanded, closing his eyes.

She had no intention of lying down next to him on the rug; she sat, cross-legged, her eyes and ears busy absorbing the forest. It wasn't silent at all; she heard the whisper of the wind among the leaves and fern, the call of birds busy nest-building or feeding their young, the scrape of branches against each other, a dog barking, a rustle of something among the leaf-mould, the whirr of insects and the hum of flies.

Then she looked at Laird and her heart beat heavily inside her ribcage; her blood ran hotly and her mouth grew dry. His eyes were still shut, the thick bar of his lashes down against his cheek, his hair given a blue-black depth in sunlight, his hard mouth relaxed and gentle as he breathed in that regular way. She ached to touch him, kiss the warm curve of that mouth, but she sat unmoving and watched him.

Laird's lovemaking wouldn't satisfy the need she felt;
he could give her passion, delight, a sensuous
pleasure, but he wouldn't give her what she needed
above everything else. Laird wouldn't love her, and
she had never been loved since she was very small,
she needed love. She wanted to be held in arms that
cared and cherished, to belong and be part of a family
again. She was so tired of being alone, living alone;
you could be strong and independent, but that didn't
make you any the less human, it didn't help you to
contemplate the emptiness of days and nights without
another human being close to you, as you needed
them.

She had thought once that her career was all she
needed; now she knew it wasn't enough, any more
than it would be enough to let Laird make love to her
when he didn't feel anything but desire.

'What are you thinking?' Laird asked softly,
opening his eyes, and she felt her colour rise.

Looking away quickly, she shrugged. 'It's beautiful
here, isn't it?'

He didn't answer, he watched her implacably,
trying to get past her hurriedly shuttered face. After
a moment, he said, 'Well, shall we have this picnic?'
and Anna was relieved to be able to get busy
unpacking the hamper.

As they ate the cold chicken legs, Laird asked,
'When did you first want to go on the stage?' and she
found that easy enough to answer. Talking shop was
the easiest thing in the world; it helped her to forget
how she felt about being alone with him. She began
to tell him about her months in the repertory
company, the parts she had played, the other actors
she had worked with.

'The leading man was incredibly good-looking, if he stood still on the stage people gasped in the stalls, but he was wood from the neck up, he couldn't act his way out of a paper bag.'

'What was his name?'

'You won't have heard of him, he's still there, acting badly. His stage name was Jago Morcar . . . '

'What?' Laird interrupted, laughing.

'I know, absurd, isn't it? His real name was Ted Brown, but he insisted on being called Jago. Mind you, it didn't seem to matter that he couldn't act—all the women were in love with him.'

'Were you?' asked Laird, watching her through narrowed eyes.

Anna laughed. 'For five minutes, after I first met him, but not once I'd seen him act. He made me laugh too much. But he was amazing to look at!'

'Have you ever really been in love?' Laird asked, and she shook her head, not meeting his eyes. She didn't want him to guess how she felt about him; he was quite capable of manipulating her feelings to his own advantage.

Laird said drily, 'Never been kissed, never been in love—anyone would think you'd spent your life in a convent. Are you sure you're twenty-two? Even Patti seems to know more about life than you do.'

'I've never been to the moon, but I know it's there,' Anna said.

His eyes narrowed. 'What does that cryptic little remark mean?'

'You don't have to experience something yourself to believe in it,' she explained.

'Blind faith, you mean?' he said cynically.

'Faith isn't blind, it just operates by rules you don't understand,' Anna told him, but the discussion was worrying her. It might tell him too much about her. 'Open the champagne,' she said. 'I'm thirsty; these game chips are rather salty, aren't they?'

'That's how the French cook them,' Laird told her absently, opening the vacuum ice bucket. 'Parsons was trained by a French chef.' He skilfully popped the cork of the champagne and poured a little into the two glasses Parsons had packed in the hamper. The wine was still cold and very refreshing; Anna tasted the fizzy dryness on her tongue with pleasure, then held out her glass for some more.

Giving her a wry smile, Laird said, 'Careful—remember how it goes to your head. I don't want you accusing me of rape again.'

'Two glasses is all I mean to have,' she said defiantly.

He smiled again, his eyes teasing. 'I'm glad to hear it.' Then he asked softly, 'Glad you came?'

Her green eyes answered him, and his smile deepened.

CHAPTER TEN

TEN DAYS later, Anna and Patti moved into the new flat, a process which, for Anna, meant only packing the two suitcases which held everything she owned in the world, while for Patti it was a good deal more complicated. A removal van was needed to convey all the furniture she had selected from her family home, along with her records, books, clothes and other personal possessions.

Naomi Montgomery offered to come to help the two girls settle into the flat, but they felt that she was busy enough with the arrangements for her own move down to Sussex, and warmly told her they could manage. Arranging everything seemed to take them hours, but the novelty made it fun, especially as they were sharing the work, and they enjoyed it enormously. As she darted around the flat, Anna almost had to pinch herself to believe she was really going to be living here. It was such a violent contrast to the place where she had been living; her whole world had altered since she met Laird and Patti.

It was very warm during those middle weeks of May; the horse-chestnut trees along the riverside had burst into bloom, great white candles of flowers rising among the fan-like green leaves. The two girls sat on their new balcony in silence and watched, entranced, as sunlight glittered on the river and in the distance Tower Bridge opened to let a ship pass underneath.

Anna sighed; she knew she would never have enough of watching that view.

'If you lean right out over the rail, you can see the turrets of the Tower,' said Patti, leaning out and craning her neck.

'If we look out at midnight, maybe we'll even see Anne Boleyn walking about with her head under her arm, like the old song.'

'What old song?' Patti asked, and Anna looked amazed.

'Don't you know it?' She began to sing it. 'With her head tucked underneath her arm, she walks the Bloody Tower . . . '

'How horrid!' Patti shuddered, then leant over the rail, waving violently. 'There's Joey—hi, Joey! Joey! He's coming to see us!'

Alarmed, Anna jumped up and pulled her backwards to safety. 'Be careful—you almost went over then! You'd better not lean over like that again, Patti. You might get vertigo.'

It hadn't escaped her that Patti was walking on air, so excited that she was flushed and euphoric as she laughed confidently.

'Of course I won't—don't fuss, you're worse than my mother!' She moved off the balcony, crossing their immaculate sitting-room, entirely furnished from Wolfstone Square, with deep blue velvet-upholstered chairs, curtains which matched the material and were only slightly and most gently faded by having been hung in the sunlight at the windows of one of the rooms in the old house, and an ivory and blue Chinese carpet. The furniture was rose-wood, early nineteenth century, Patti said. 'Not really valuable,' she denied when Anna looked somewhat alarmed. 'Pretty, but there's a lot of it about.' Anna had not been too reassured.

She was still disturbed by the private earthquake which had exploded into her life, made rubble of the familiar landmarks and removed her to an entirely unknown neighbourhood.

Patti was opening the door to Joey Ross who was carrying a large bunch of white and purple lilac. The scent filled the entire flat and both Anna and Patti glowed with delight in it. The delicate, heady fragrance brought summer into the flat; the tiny bells of flowerets crowded together among the green, smooth leaves, so profusely that it was as if Joey was carrying a little lilac tree.

'How lovely,' Patti said, burying her face in the flowers. 'Where did you get it?'

'I picked it in my garden,' Joey told her, wandering around the flat like a prowling cat inspecting a strange house, his hands in the pockets of his black leather jacket. Watching him, Anna thought that there was something distinctly feline about Joey: an almost malicious intelligence in his quick, darting eyes with their golden-rayed pupils and a fastidious self-obsession which cared more about his own comfort and feelings than those of anyone else.

Patti carried the lilac into the kitchen to find vases for it, and Anna asked, 'Where do you live, Joey?'

'Hampstead.' He picked up a piece of porcelain and turned it over, inspecting the mark on the base. 'Dear me—Bow,' he said, admiring the blue and white glaze. 'Yours or Patti's?'

'Patti's,' Anna said drily, and Joey gave her an ironic smile.

'I hope this is going to work.'

'You and me both,' Anna said. 'Do you live in a flat or a house?'

'I've got the ground floor of a large house—and the garden, although the owner employs a gardener to keep that in trim.'

Patti came back with a cup of coffee for Joey in one hand, a shopping basket in the other.

'I'm going shopping,' she said with enthusiasm. 'We need all sorts of things. You stay and chat to Joey, it won't take me long. I'll go to those shops in the arcade. Anything I can get you?'

Anna shook her head, her face wry. She and Joey watched Patti rushing away as if she had wings on her feet, their eyes meeting as the front door banged.

'She makes me feel very old,' Anna groaned, and Joey laughed.

'I'd say she's having a rush of freedom to the head.'

'I'm afraid you're right,' she agreed ruefully.

'Well, her family have kept her pretty close to home until now! I suppose it was a phase she was bound to go through, sooner or later. Old Montgomery is rather old to be the father of a girl of her age; his ideas are almost Edwardian. I'm surprised they didn't try to persuade her to go to university, though.'

'I don't think she wanted to go. Patti has strong ideas about what she does or doesn't want. If she'd gone to college—whether it was university or drama school—she'd have tasted freedom a long time ago. She has a lot of catching up to do, but she'll sort it all out in her mind in time.'

'Have you got a fill-in job yet?' Joey asked as he put down his cup, and Anna shook her head. 'Well, I'll keep my eyes and ears open. Don't worry, we'll find you something to do until we start rehearsing for the West End run.' He got to his feet. 'Now, before I rush off, can I see this famous view of the river and Tower Bridge?'

Anna showed him out of the french windows on to the balcony and they stood there, gazing along the water in silence. Joey turned his head to smile down into her eyes.

'OK, you're right—it is fabulous, and I'm green with envy. Amazing to remember that only a few years ago this whole area was a rotting maze of warehouses and docks, isn't it? I remember filming down here seven years ago—just ten minutes from this building, in fact. Did you ever see the TV version of the life of Dickens? I worked on that, doing theatre research for the director. This part of the riverside still reeked of Dickens, it didn't seem to have changed since he was a boy. Now it's altering fast.'

'Some of the other flats are still vacant,' Anna told him. 'If you're interested?'

'I don't know if I can afford it,' he shrugged. He put a hand up to her windblown red-gold hair, brushing it back from her eyes. 'You know, I might get you some modelling—how do you feel about that?'

'It's better than working as a waitress!'

He laughed, pinching her ear. 'Is that the alternative? Well, I'll see what I can do—I've got a lot of friends in advertising and photography. They owe me favours.'

As Anna opened the door to show him out they found themselves facing Laird, wintry-faced and aloof in a formal pin-striped city suit.

'Oh, hi,' said Joey, startled and showing it.

Laird nodded, sparing no words on him, his profile rigidly arctic. It was lucky Joey couldn't see his eyes which were hidden by those heavy lids as he let the other man pass. Anna saw them a second later as the lids lifted and Laird looked directly at her. The grey eyes were molten, seething with a desire to do violence. Anna's throat closed up at the sight of them.

Turning back to her, Joey said, 'Well, I'll start ringing my old pals and see what they can chase up for you. Don't worry, Anna. I'll get you some sort of work.'

'Thank you,' she said, without being quite sure what she was saying. Her mind couldn't concentrate on Joey Ross; she was too intensely aware of Laird's silent rage, resenting it and yet trembling at it. He never ceased to surprise her; she had just become convinced that he was as charming and kind and fascinating as she had first thought in his penthouse before she got too drunk to know what was going on—and now the hardness and iciness was back in his face. Why? she asked herself, stepping back into the flat and closing the door on Joey's departing back.

Laird had walked into the sitting-room and was standing in it like a general surveying a battlefield from a hill; his mouth set, his eyes grim.

'Where's Patti?' he grated.

'Out shopping, she should be back soon,' Anna told him in a voice she tried to keep firm and calm, without too much success.

'Alone?'

The snarl of his voice made her jump and flush. 'She's not a child, you know, and it is broad daylight —why shouldn't she go shopping alone?'

'And you were here with Ross,' he sneered, his mouth full of contempt. 'Alone! And you're not a child, either, and what you do is your business, but don't involve Patti in your fun and games.'

'Fun and games? What are you accusing me of now?' Anna was incredulous. 'Joey and I were talking.'

He laughed shortly. 'Oh, is that what you were doing?'

'Yes, it was!'

'Out on the balcony a few minutes ago?' He made the question sound like a trap and Anna stammered back, flustered and uncertain, not sure what he meant.

'What are you talking about?'

'He was touching you. Stroking your hair, your face . . . is that your idea of conversation?'

She just stared at him, then a smile crept into her eyes. 'Are you jealous?'

Laird stared fixedly at her for a long moment, his face confused, darkly flushed, frowning, then he turned on his heel and walked out on to the balcony and stood there with his back to her, staring down over the river. Anna slowly walked out after him and watched his profile; the afternoon sun gave her a clear view of every pore, every line, every angle.

Without looking at her, Laird said huskily, 'I'll never marry again, I couldn't risk it. I got too mauled last time, she chewed me up and spat me out, and it took me years to recover. No, that's not even the truth. You never *do* recover from something like that, especially if it follows on from a traumatic child-hood.' He gripped the rail of the balcony with both hands, his knuckles whitening with the pressure of that grasp, and leaned over, his head bent and the wind whipping through the thick dark hair.

Anna watched him with a strange intensity, her eyes glowing with passion and compassion. As if she had known him then, she picked up his suffering and hated the two women who had caused it.

'My mother was very beautiful—I've inherited her colouring but not her looks, she really was lovely, and of course, I adored her. Boys are always romantic creatures, even when they do their best to hide it. I was fond of my father, too, but not with the same strong feeling. After she'd gone, I felt guilty, as if it was my fault, I'd done something wrong, I'd let her down . . . it never even occurred to me that it had nothing to do with me, that she probably hardly knew I existed. No, I was so self-centred then that I took all the blame and all the guilt, and for a long, long time I was utterly miserable. Eventually, of course, I came out of it and began to hate her—that was far healthier and I soon recovered after that, but it left scars, and when Merieth started having affairs I had a terrible sense of *déjà vu*.'

He sighed, his shoulders heaving, and Anna asked huskily, 'You didn't blame yourself for that, too?'

'God knows. With my head, no! But we don't always use our heads at crisis points; we revert to using our instincts, without even knowing what we're doing. My unconscious fished it all up from my childhood; I started confusing my wife and my mother and between rage and unhappiness I no longer knew what I really felt or thought. When Merieth went, I was relieved because it was over, what I suppose I'd always dreaded had happened—my marriage had broken up, just like my father's, my wife had gone, just like my mother, and left me with a lot of questions and no answers.'

'What questions?' asked Anna, frowning, angry with him for hurting himself like this and wanting to make him see how crazy it was to feel guilt over the past for so many years.

He straightened, shrugging, and stared fixedly at the distant roofscape of London's riverside, the warehouses and modern office blocks, the spires and towers.

'About myself, about women, about the impossibility of ever being happy with one of them.'

Anna felt her body turn to ice, a chill echo sounding in her ears. His voice had a flat inevitability, a finality that left no room for hope or doubt or question.

'Or even loving one,' Laird said in that distant tone. 'Liking one, maybe. Even wanting one. I haven't turned into a monk or gone in for voluntary chastity, I'm not saying that. But I'm simply not prepared to risk letting myself in for that again.'

Anna didn't think she would be able to speak because her throat was so raw with pain, but she forced her tongue to move, to make sounds, to say what she wanted to say. 'All women aren't . . . '

He didn't let her finish. 'No, of course, I know! But . . . ' He turned and she saw his face for the first time, flinching from it and fighting down the tears which rose to her eyes. Laird looked at her almost as if in desperation, 'It makes no difference, you see. I'm too terrified of getting hurt again, like a rider who's been thrown and broken too many bones ever to get on the back of a horse again—I know I couldn't face it.'

Anna tried to think, to marshal arguments, to talk calmly and sanely, but she could only feel, and what she felt was a pain like his; a terrible, aching sadness and hopelessness.

'Have you ever tried?' she whispered, and he smiled, a brief, wry twist of the mouth more than a real smile.

'Oh, yes.'

Anna winced and he watched her, frowning, as if he could see in her face the jealousy that had stabbed through her at the idea of Laird trying to love other women.

'It never worked out,' he said. 'Each time the same thing happened—oh, not that the woman left me for another man, but each time I got so far and couldn't go on, I had to stop seeing her in case I did feel anything. I'd start getting the sort of panic you feel when you look down from a great height. I was on the Eiffel Tower once when I saw a woman staring down and you could see from her face how terrified she was, she had to be helped down, she was in such a state. That's how I feel about loving a woman.'

'Why are you telling *me* all this?' she asked, and he gave an unsteady little smile.

'You know why, don't you, Anna?'

She did, of course. He was telling her because he knew she was in love with him, and he was warning her off. Being cruel to be kind, she thought wildly, staring at him.

'You were right—I was jealous when I saw you with Ross on the balcony,' he said, with a rough groan. 'I was jealous when I saw him kiss you in his car a few weeks back. That's part of the trouble; as soon as I even think of falling in love I become impossibly possessive, jealous, suspicious.' He walked back into the sitting-room and prowled up and down like a caged animal, pacing from wall to wall and back, avoiding furniture with the neatness of a bat flying in the dark. 'That isn't my usual state of mind, and I hate feeling like that, I don't seem able to help myself.'

Anna walked back into the room, but stood by the windows watching his restless wandering.

'You're beautiful, Anna,' he said roughly. 'And I'm attracted to you, we both know that, so we might as well be frank. I want you, but I have to be honest with you. I don't want to have an affair with you and then have you turn round and accuse me of cheating you. I'm a burnt-out case, Anna. I haven't got any love to give you. Love costs too much.'

She looked around the room, away from him, her face hot, then as cold as ice. 'Did I ask you to love me?'

He was suddenly still, watching her. 'Doesn't it matter?' he asked huskily, and she was so busy fighting down the pain she felt that she didn't understand what he was saying until he moved and she felt his arms going round her. 'Anna,' he whispered, his mouth hunting hers. 'I want you so badly, you've been driving me crazy for weeks!'

She shuddered as she felt that touch, the seeking warmth of the lips moving over her cheek, kissing her ears, her throat, looking hungrily for the mouth she was averting while she tried to think.

He was offering her passion and sensuality but not love; and he might satisfy the craving she had been fighting for weeks, he might give her a physical pleasure she knew she needed from him, but it would never be enough. It wouldn't mean a thing if Laird couldn't love her, *wouldn't* love her. She had understood what he was really saying a moment ago—Laird had been obliquely admitting that he had been on the verge of falling in love with her, but was pulling back from the edge, refusing to let it happen, and Anna was angry with him. That was far worse than if he had never felt a thing.

She pushed him away, shaking her head. 'No. I won't have an affair with you, let go of me!' The fierceness in her voice got home to him and he stood, staring down at her, his hands falling.

'Do you think you're the only one who's afraid of getting hurt?' she muttered. 'You're still self-obsessed, Laird, or you might realise that nothing excuses you for hurting someone else—especially deliberately, with your eyes wide open, knowing what you're doing.'

He looked taken aback, frowning, darkly flushed, his eyes restless. 'That's just it, I don't want to hurt you,' he said impatiently.

'You think by telling me in advance that it may hurt, you're absolved from all guilt when it does?'

He grimaced. 'You think that's what I was doing?'

'Wasn't it?'

He swung and walked away, his head bent as he thought about that.

Anna said flatly, 'I have my life worked out, Laird. I planned it all years ago, when I was still at school. I suppose you could say I believe in my destiny—it's the only way you ever get anything, by believing you will. I'm going to be a famous actress and I don't want to wreck my chances by giving too much of myself to a relationship that has no future anyway. You said you wanted to be honest, so let's be honest. I could fall in love with you and ruin my life, or I could send you away and get on with my career. Which do you think would be wisest?'

He gave her a cool, ironic stare. 'Yes, I get the point. I hadn't looked at it from your angle—I'd just told myself that that was what I was doing.'

'You were making excuses for yourself in advance!'

'OK, don't rub it in. You're right.' He came back and smiled down into her eyes with all the charm she now resented. 'I do have one cast-iron excuse for myself—you really are lovely and I'm not going to apologise for wanting you.' He held out a hand, eyes rueful. 'Friends?'

Anna shook her head. 'Do you think that would work? Because I don't. Stay away from me, Laird, please. I won't be your mistress and I can't be your friend, so just stay away.'

His hand dropped, he stared at her as if bewildered, then turned and walked out of the flat, banging the door behind him. He was angry with her because she had made him see the plain truth. He was angry with her because she wouldn't let him have his cake and eat it. If she hadn't sent him away altogether, he would have kept trying to seduce her into bed with him, and she was too much in love to be sure of her own will-power. He might have succeeded one day, and that would have been a disaster for her.

She was achingly sorry for him; Laird was in an emotional muddle and hurting himself as much as anyone else. But she had to protect herself; she had already suffered enough over him, she couldn't bear any more.

CHAPTER ELEVEN

THE PLAY'S run ended a fortnight later and the cast separated with a mixture of regret and relief; some of them would meet again when rehearsals began for the West End run, but the others were either still hunting for new jobs or had been lucky enough to get work and eager to start. All of them had enjoyed doing the play, but they were all looking forward to a rest from the daily performances. Long runs were tiring and in the end could be boring; they hadn't reached that stage quite yet, but Dame Flossie said she had begun to get restless.

'I'm going away to the sun for a few weeks, dears. See you in July,' she said at the party to celebrate the last night, and later asked Anna if she had fixed up any work yet.

'My agent says there's nothing around, but Joey is sending me along to an advertising agency on Monday. They're looking for someone to do a TV commercial. Lots of competition, of course, but who knows? I might be lucky, it's worth a try.'

'Oh, always have to go, darling, you don't know what you can do until you've tried,' Dame Flossie agreed.

Patti was going down to Sussex to spend two weeks with her parents since she would not be starting at the drama school until the new term in September, and she felt like spending some time in the country.

'Come with me, there's plenty of room,' she had told Anna, who had been tempted but after a struggle with herself had refused, very regretfully. Her rent for the riverside flat was heavily subsidised by the Montgomery family; she did not want to accept any more at their hands.

'I'd better stay in town in case I get a call from my agent,' she excused herself, and Patti grimaced.

'I suppose so. It would have been fun, though. Will you come down and visit at weekends, Anna? There are fast trains and we'll meet you at the station in Hastings and drive you to the village, and get you back.'

'I'll try,' Anna conceded, but secretly she preferred not to run the risk of seeing Laird on one of these weekends. 'I'll let you know,' she added hurriedly. 'At the moment I don't know what I'll be doing.'

She had not set eyes on Laird since the warm May afternoon when they quarrelled in the flat. Anna had told him to stay away from her and he had obviously taken her at her word. She kept telling herself it was a great relief, she didn't want to see him, but she knew she lied.

She had missed him every minute of every day and ached to see him—just once, even at a distance. It disturbed her to hunger for a glimpse of him, but she couldn't reason herself out of it. He had embedded himself under her skin, a sharp, nagging thorn, she could not cut out. The harder she tried, the deeper she seemed to drive it.

Patti left for Sussex on Sunday, catching a train before lunch, and Anna had the flat to herself for the first time. The pleasure she felt was a little spoilt because it rained all that afternoon, but on the

Monday the weather turned hot and humid. For her visit to the advertising agency she wore a new white cotton dress, crisp and cool and elegantly styled. She wore her hair casually but had spent a long time coaxing it into exactly the shape she wanted, and her long, slim legs looked their best in filmy nylons. Her fragile white high-heeled sandals were Patti's; she had lent them to Anna for the occasion, and they were perfect with the new dress.

As she had expected, there was a number of other girls waiting in the reception area, all of them looking more glamorous than Anna felt. Their eyes skimmed over her hurriedly, shrewdly, assessing her as a threat. They gave her bright, false smiles, tension in the lines around their eyes and mouths. Anna hated that aspect of her profession—auditions, competition, the emotional see-saw of hope and rejection. The room reverberated with nerves scraped raw, the voices too lively, the faces unconvincingly cheerful.

Why do we do it? she brooded as she sat on the rather hard chair, her body assuming a smooth pose which was far from relaxing. From time to time someone would wander past into an inner room in which the interviews were being held and all the girls would sit up, smiling, willing the man to notice them. One by one the girls were called. Anna felt like going home when her name was suddenly called and she got up, flustered, dropping the folder of photographs and press notices that her agent had told her to bring along.

The interview was short and, she found, humiliating. The three men behind the desk looked at her folder, asked her questions, made her stand up and turn around, asked her to walk across the room, then back, and stared and stared in a way which set her teeth on edge.

'Well, we'll test you,' one of them said, a pencil between his teeth, flicking over the pages of a thick diary. 'Let's see . . . the studio is free on Thursday at three. OK for you?'

'Yes,' Anna said at once. 'What will you want me to do?'

'We'll tell you then. Wear casuals—jeans will do, or dungarees. We'll supply the clothes for the actual filming, of course, but we'd like to get an idea of how you look in casual gear.'

'What sort of commercial is it?' asked Anna.

'Didn't your agent tell you? Oh, no, Joey Ross suggested you, didn't he?' The men glanced at each other, grinning in a way Anna resented. 'The product's unimportant. We're just going to test you to find out if you're photogenic. Three o'clock, Thursday, at our studios—the secretary outside will give you the address. Don't be late or you'll miss your chance. We have a lot of tests to do that day.'

On the way back to her flat Anna pondered on the grin the men had exchanged—had they decided that Joey was pushing her because she was his latest girl-friend? She should have realised people might jump to that conclusion.

It was annoying to know they thought that, but it wasn't true, so it didn't really matter, she told herself, but in spite of that it niggled, and she was in a defensive, uptight mood on the following Thursday when she went along to the studio at which she was to be tested. It had been a considerable relief to be told to wear casual clothes, since she had little else; she had put on jeans and a cotton T-shirt, getting a number of glances from men in the street as she walked past. Anna ignored them all, eaten with nerves over the test she was to do.

There was a very pretty girl at the reception desk in the studio. She gave Anna a stare as sweet as icecream and as cold.

'Can I help you?'

'I'm here to do a film test,' Anna mentioned the name of the man who had sent her and the girl continued to stare, picking up the telephone with one hand.

'Mr Tomkins? She's here.'

Anna heard the voice at the other end asked brusquely, 'Who?'

'The girl for the Montgomery test,' the receptionist said.

Anna turned to stone on the spot. From a long distance she heard the receptionist talking; Anna just stared at her pink mouth moving, as if she was trying to lip-read.

The girl got up, behind her desk, backing with an alarmed expression on her face. Suddenly her voice came into Anna's ears, which had been deaf for a long time.

'Look, are you crazy or something?'

That was when Anna heard herself muttering. 'Bastard, bastard . . . ' She shut her mouth hurriedly and turned and ran, leaving the receptionist gazing after her, no doubt with relief.

Anna only had one idea in her head; she wanted to get to the Mongomery building and get her hands round his throat and squeeze until he stopped breathing. How dared he set that up? No wonder the two advertising agency men had grinned at each

other. They weren't guessing, they *knew* that Laird
Montgomery had fixed it for her to get a TV
commercial, and she couldn't blame them for
thinking his reasons were purely personal, because
Anna knew they were. Laird was still trying to buy
her. The price kept going up; she ought to be flat-
tered about that. First red roses, then a luxury flat
and now a part in a TV commercial. For his firm, of
course! They didn't normally advertise on television,
or, at least, she had never seen an advertisement
—had he set one up simply to trap her? It would be
an expensive business for him, but then Laird was
rich, he could afford to indulge his whims.

How dared he? she thought again with yearning
violence. I'll kill him. How many other people know
now? The people at the advertising agency, at the
studio . . . they'll talk, of course. They're bound
to! It would get around and a gossip columnist might
pick it up and print it. Oh, God, I'll kill him, Anna
promised herself, as she jumped into a taxi and gave
the address of his office building.

Traffic was heavy, people making their way back
to their offices after late lunches sat in taxis simmering
with irritation, one eye on a watch while they stared
at the other taxis jammed in around them. It took
Anna half an hour to get to Laird's office block.

She shot through the huge plate-glass doors and
was at once confronted by a man in gold-braided
uniform. 'Can I help you, miss?'

'I want to see Mr Montgomery,' Anna told him
through her teeth.

She was surprised when he did not seem surprised.
'Yes, miss,' he told her blandly. 'Will you come this
way?'

Suspiciously Anna followed him across the marble floor, her footsteps echoing and bouncing off marble walls and a high, white ceiling, into a lift. She watched him press the button. They were going to the floor just below the penthouse, all right. The lift shot upwards and Anna frowned, her mind working at the speed of light.

Her arrival was not unexpected. Laird had known she would come here. How? Her eyes hunted around the lift, her brows knitted. Of course, the studio must have rung the advertising agency and they must have rung Laird and he had guessed she would rush round here, burning with fury. He had told his doorman to watch for her and bring her to him. It was another trap!

'I've changed my mind,' she said to the startled doorman, her hand shooting out to press the button for the ground floor.

'Careful, miss!' the man said, barring her way.

'I want to go back down!'

The lift doors opened and Laird stood there. Anna backed away into the furthest corner of the lift. 'Will you please take me down again?' she said coldly to the doorman.

He was already walking out of the lift in obedience to Laird's jerk of the head. Anna leapt to the button panel, but too late. Laird was in the lift with her and the lift doors were closing.

'I will not go to the penthouse!' she hissed between her teeth.

Laird's hand hovered over the button; he stared at her, those grey eyes darkened with some emotion, the black pupils dilated and glittering. He was in his formal city clothes—dark jacket, pinstriped trousers, highly polished black shoes, a dark tie on a crisp white shirt. He looked expensive and exclusive and a million light years out of her orbit. She wished she had never met him; she dragged her eyes away from him because it hurt to look at him.

'Either we talk in the penthouse or my office —make up your mind!' he said, and the deep tones of his voice did something drastic to her heartbeat.

'Don't give me orders!' she muttered, her eyes lowered so that she wouldn't be exposed to the danger of seeing him.

'You came here to see me. What did you want to say?' He sounded so cool; the bare-faced effrontery almost took her breath away. Almost, but not quite.

'You know very well what I came here to say!' she burst out, shaking with fury. 'How could you do it? I've never been so humiliated in my life!'

'I only wanted to help!' Laird said, and the defensive note in his voice did nothing to soothe her, but while she was choosing the right words to throw back at him, the lift suddenly began to move.

Anna lurched sideways and Laird caught her, his arm going round her waist. She slapped his hand down, fizzing with rage.

'What did you do? Where's the lift going?'

He looked up at the illuminated numerals above the door. 'Down,' he said drily. 'Somebody must have rung for it on a lower floor.'

As he said that the lift came to a halt, the doors opened and two men walked in, glancing at Laird and hurriedly smiling.

'Afternoon, sir.' They were obviously surprised to see him.

Laird answered calmly, and the lift moved down again to the ground floor. The two men politely stood back to let Laird walk out first, but he shook his head.

'I'm going back up.'

Anna started to walk forward; he grabbed the belt of her jeans and held on to it, his hand hidden behind her back.

'We're both going back up,' he told the men, who were looking at her uncertainly. They left the lift and Laird leaned forward to press a button; the doors closed and the lift set off again.

Anna could feel Laird's cool fingers in the small of her back, their tips brushing her naked spine. 'Will you let go of me?' she asked icily, pulling. He let go of her belt.

'Anna, I had the purest motives,' he said quietly, and she laughed incredulously.

'What? You don't really expect me to believe that—after your other attempts to buy me?'

'That was before I knew you,' he said as the lift stopped again and the doors opened. She knew they were on the penthouse floor before she saw the familiar corridor.

'If we're going to talk, we'll talk in your office,' she said, moving towards the panel to take them down there, but Laird was too quick for her. He rushed her, as if this was a rugby scrum, took hold of her waist and lifted her out bodily, kicking uselessly, but with such force that Laird lost his footing and they both sprawled on the corridor carpet. He fell on top of her, his weight pinning her there, breathless and infuriated.

They both heard the whine of the lift descending. Laird raised himself, his hands flat on the carpet, staring down at her with a look in his eyes that made Anna's throat close up in dangerous excitement and alarm.

'Get up,' she said hoarsely, knowing she was trembling and he must feel it as his body held her down in that forced intimacy.

Laird's eyes were glittering, half veiled by those heavy lids, a dark flush on his face. He looked into her own eyes, a half-smile on his mouth, then slowly his stare drifted down over her face to the quivering curve of her parted lips.

'No,' Anna whispered, wanting him to kiss her so badly that she could have killed him.

'You're so beautiful,' he said huskily.

She shut her eyes, ice-cold. 'I won't be your mistress, Laird.'

'And I can't let you go,' he said, grimacing at her. 'I've missed you like hell, Anna. And worried about you, all alone in the flat while Patti's with my parents—why wouldn't you go to Sussex, too? I could have slept better if I'd known you were safe down there, but I stayed awake until the early hours every night wondering if anything was happening to you, imagining the flat being burgled, some vicious swine attacking you. You read about this sort of thing without registering what it means. It started to haunt me when I thought of it happening to you.'

'I've managed to look after myself since I was sixteen and first came to London,' she retorted.

'My God! The risks you've taken!'

'There's risk in most things, you can't lock yourself up and throw away the key just to avoid taking risks!'

'I can't bear to think of it,' Laird groaned, his hand stroking the tumbled red-gold hair which had spilled across the carpet. 'Patti told me you hadn't managed to fix up any work and that worried me even more. I had to do something, surely you can see that? It was a simple matter—I wasn't giving you anything, just arranging for you to get a job! Why are you so angry?'

She looked at him, despairing of getting it home to him. 'You think money fixes anything, buys anything!'

'That isn't fair, Anna. I wasn't trying to buy you, not this time, not ever. I asked you to live with me; I never mentioned money.'

'You didn't have to, did you? You dangled a luxury apartment in front of me and a luxury life to go with it—nothing so sordid as hard cash, of course, but it was a form of barter. You gave me all that and in return I slept with you.' Her voice was harsh and bitter, her face white now. 'What would you call that, Laird? I call it trying to buy me.'

His eyes were confused and restless, his colour high. 'Only if you didn't . . . ' He broke off, and she watched him intently.

'If I didn't what?'

He swallowed, hesitating. 'Want me,' he said at last, but she knew with a leap of intuition that that was not what he had been going to say.

'Wanting is easy,' Anna said softly. 'Loving is hard.'

Laird met her eyes, looked away, a muscle jerking beside his jaw. She waited breathlessly for him to say something, and at that moment the door of the penthouse suite opened and they heard a voice which made Laird close his eyes and groan.

'A nice way to carry on, I must say!'

Laird got to his feet, brushing a hand over his elegant suit, and turned to eye Parsons crushingly.

'We tripped.'

'Go on!' Parsons retorted with a sneer. 'I wasn't born yesterday.'

'Or even in this century,' Laird jeered back, helping Anna to her feet. Very pink, she kept her eyes down.

'Oh, charming. If you was wanting me to cook anything, that's tough. I'm just on me way out to see the doctor. I've got my bad back again.'

'Don't bother to hurry back,' Laird told him, taking Anna by the elbow and steering her into the penthouse.

Parsons cackled and Anna flushed, feeling Laird watching her. He slammed the front door on the old man. 'Damn him!'

'You can't blame him for what he's thinking,' Anna muttered, walking into the sitting-room and over to the window. 'He's not so far wrong, is he? You've been trying to seduce me ever since I met you.'

'I wasn't trying this time—the TV commercial is a genuine no-strings offer! We'd been planning it for some time. The director the agency picked out wanted a new face, an actress, not a model; someone with what he calls instant impact. They were running through a list of possibilities and I thought—why not you? I suggested they test you, and that's all I did!'

She laughed bitterly, turning to face him. 'They weren't likely to refuse, though, were they now?'

He scowled at her. 'You were ready to let Joey Ross pull strings for you, why not me?'

'Was Joey in on this too?' Anna was shaken as she realised he must have been. It was Joey who had told her to visit the advertising agency!

Laird's narrowed eyes noted the change in her expression and his frown deepened. 'What exactly is going on between you and Ross?' he demanded.

Anna did not bother to answer that, she asked in her turn: 'Did Joey know you'd set it up? He co-operated with you?' That shocked her, she wouldn't have believed it of Joey. He was a maddening man, but she had always thought he was as straight as a die.

Laird swung away, prowling restlessly back and forth, his hands in his jacket pockets. 'No, he had no idea I was involved. He'd been ringing around trying to find work for you and the agency who handles our account was one of those he contacted. They got back to him and told him to send you along to see them. I told them not to mention my name.'

Anna's mouth twisted. 'You're so damn devious!' Yet she was relieved to hear that Joey hadn't been part of the plot.

Laird halted in front of her, his eyes hard and fixed. 'Is Ross in love with you?'

Anna considered, briefly, the idea of lying to him—it might end this whole tangle if she did. On the other hand it would complicate an already complex situation and it would be embarrassing if Joey ever found out. What on earth would she say to him?

'Well? Is he?' Laird insisted harshly, and she shook her head. At once Laird's face relaxed and a little smile of satisfaction curved his mouth. She could have screamed as she saw it—Laird didn't love her himself, yet at the bare idea that someone else might care for her he was ready to snarl and show his teeth in a display of jealousy to which he had no right whatever.

'Sit down, Anna,' he said softly, still smiling.

She shook her head fiercely. 'I'm going in a minute—I only came to make it clear that I wasn't accepting your help, whether there are strings attached to it or not! In future, please stay out of my life and let me solve my own problems!'

'If you were prepared to accept Ross's help, why can't you accept mine?' he asked, moving towards her.

She whirled towards the door, afraid of the look in his eyes. 'Because I can't!'

Laird got to the door before her and barred her way, leaning negligently against the doorframe, that long-limbed body deceptively casual. His eyes were far from casual; Anna watched them tensely like someone faced with a wild creature, a sleek black panther, purring in its throat and crouched in apparent drowsiness while it waited to spring and kill.

'Why can't you?' he probed in that husky voice. 'You need that job.'

'Not that much!'

His brows lifted. 'No? What will you do instead? Live on social security?'

'Get a job as a waitress. I've done it before, I can do it again. I can move out of Patti's flat, too, and find somewhere I can afford. I won't take any more charity from you. You keep telling me there are no strings attached, but for some reason I don't believe you.'

He frowned impatiently, his mouth a straight line, holding her eyes as if he was trying to penetrate through them to the inmost recesses of her mind. Anna defended her privacy, dropping her lids, hiding her thoughts and emotions from him as much as she could. Laird used any weapon he could get hold of; he was unscrupulous and far too clever, as well as having more charm than was good for one man to possess. This time she was not succumbing to his charm; he wouldn't get anywhere with her if he gave her one of those sidelong, coaxing smiles.

'I'm not offering you charity! You're doing my family a favour by living with Patti, and as for taking a job as a waitress—I won't hear of that, it would be far too tiring for you. You've been working hard in the theatre for months, you need a few weeks' rest, not an even tougher job for even lower pay.'

Anna lifted her eyes and gave him a straight, tired stare. 'Laird, what I do is no business of yours. Can't you get that through your head? My life is my own affair.'

He seemed to have no answer to that, although his bones had locked into a tense mask.

'So will you please get out of my way and let me leave?' she asked into that grim silence.

He was the one who was looking down now; his body had a weary pose, his head hanging, his hands at his side, his limbs slack.

Anna waited a moment, and when he still said nothing she repeated her request. 'Laird, I want to leave!'

'Don't go, Anna,' he whispered, and her body froze in shock at the note in his voice.

She looked incredulously at him; he had sounded so different, his voice unsteady, pleading.

'It scares the life out of me,' he muttered, still not looking at her and his face so pale it made every line stand out; the fine laughter lines around eye and mouth, the slash between his brows, the blackness of his lashes and brows. That face had become familiar territory to her long ago; her eyes hunted over it in search of the meaning of this change in him, but she was bewildered into asking:

'What scares you? The idea of me being a waitress? That's silly.'

His mouth twisted, he gave a soft groan. 'Not that. Feeling the way I do about you—that's what scares me. I can't cope with it, Anna. If I let myself care, and it all comes to pieces in my hands, I'll go crazy.'

Her breathing had gone haywire, she couldn't get a word out, listening with an intensity that matched the strained harshness in his voice.

'You were right a few moment ago when you said that loving is harder,' Laird said huskily. 'It's the hardest thing in the world. It means giving too much of yourself; it leaves you wide open to getting hurt.'

'But it's the same for all of us, Laird,' she said gently, aching for the sadness in his voice. 'What do you want—to be different from every other human being who ever lived? Take love out of the human being, and what's left? Just an animal with a brain.'

He eyed her through his lashes, his face darkly flushed. 'You're not afraid to risk it?'

'Yes, terrified,' she said frankly. 'Just as I'm sick every night before I go on stage—the panic gets worse while I'm waiting in the wings for my first cue. I always think I won't be able to go on—but every night, I do.'

'If you'll take the chance, I will,' he said offhandedly, not looking at her, and Anna stared at his rigid profile, her heartbeat so fast it scared her.

'Are you trying to say . . . '

'Yes,' he muttered, a muscle jerking beside his jaw. 'I'm still scared stiff, but I'd rather be scared with you than without you. I've missed you badly. I must see you, Anna. I've got to. You're always in my head, and if it's going to hurt one day . . . well, to hell with it.' He wasn't looking at her and he was still afraid to say, 'I love you', but she knew what she was hearing and her blood sang in her ears.

Anna watched him passionately as his head came up and he stared into her eyes, reading the emotions in them easily now that she had stopped trying to hide them. She put her arms around his neck and lifted her lips, saying what he wanted to hear even though he could see it in her face. 'I love you, too.' The words only just got out as his mouth crushed down on hers and he held her so tightly she could barely breathe, their bodies merging in one warm, flowing, pulsating line, breast to breast, hip to hip, thigh to thigh, their mouths mingling in hungry exploration.

Laird swept her off her feet a few moments later and carried her through to the bedroom in which she had already spent one night—that night which had begun it all just a few months earlier. Anna was quite conscious now of what he was doing, even though her eyes were half closed and drowsy with excited anticipation and the heated arousal of the last few minutes.

Laird laid her down gently and knelt beside her, stroking her ruffled hair. 'I've wanted you for so long I'm scared of my own feelings!' he muttered, his eyes busy as they ran over the clinging cotton T-shirt and the tight blue jeans. 'You're so beautiful, Anna; I can't believe I'm the first man in your life. What did you do to keep them all at bay, the wolves who must have prowled around you?'

'I told them to get lost,' she said lightly. 'I have a way with wolves.'

'I know, I noticed. I could tell I wasn't the first to chase you, just as I could tell you'd never been caught.' He eyed her mockingly. 'Until now.'

Anna laughed, then her eyes became anxious as she watched his hard-boned face. Was she crazy to think of loving him when he was still a dyed-in-the-wool cynic, a man who found it impossible to trust a woman? Did he really love her, or was he trying another trick? Was this just a new trap to get her into bed with him? He hadn't actually said he loved her, had he? She had been touched by the way he muttered incoherently, never quite saying the words she ached to hear. She had jumped to the conclusion that that was what he meant, but had she been wrong?

Laird was kissing her neck, his eyes closed, his hands moving, searching, caressing. Anna lay still and cold with apprehension, and after a moment he lifted his head again to look into her face, frowning.

'What is it? What's wrong?'

'Tell me you love me,' she said huskily. 'Before . . . I need to know if you do, Laird.'

The grey eyes glowed with a feeling she had never seen in them before, a passionate tenderness. 'I just told you I did.'

'You didn't say it.'

'Didn't I? A last supersition, I suppose. They're difficult words to say.' He groaned, closing his eyes, very flushed. 'I love you,' he said very fast, and Anna's breath caught. Laird opened his eyes again and looked at her fiercely, and she would never need to hear him say those words again because the feeling was there in his eyes. Laird had dammed up all that love for years; it had been there hidden, locked away, out of sight, behind the cynicism and the bitter wariness. Now it was visible, the dam broken, the emotion pouring out towards her in a tidal wave.

'I love you,' he said again with a husky triumph. 'Oh, Anna . . . '

Their mouths met, clung, their bodies straining together as if trying to break the bonds that separated them physically so that they could merge and become one. That instant chemical attraction had bedevilled her life ever since she met him outside the theatre; he had knocked her off her feet then and she had never quite recovered her balance. Now she knew she would never be the same again.

'I knew I'd had it when I started thinking it would be fun to marry you,' Laird said a little later, and Anna's lips parted in disbelief. 'I told myself the idea was crazy,' he went on, 'but I kept on thinking about it. I didn't think I'd ever be able to trust a woman again, but then I hadn't reckoned with someone like you. You're a one-off. Look at the way you jumped to the conclusion that I'd slept with you that night—I was staggered. I couldn't believe that any girl could be that dumb in the days of sex education in schools.'

'I was never listening,' Anna admitted. 'It all seemed so mechanical and ugly—and pretty silly, too. We used to giggle so much I hardly heard a word the teacher said.'

'I can see you need some more private lessons,' Laird murmured.

'And you were furious about my mistake!' she said hurriedly as he set about giving her a lesson.

'Only because you thought I was capable of such a lowdown trick. I found your innocence rather touching.' He watched her turning pink again, smiling at her tenderly. 'You react to everthing with such passion and intensity, I love that, too. You make me feel protective, even when you're yelling at me or slapping me down over my rather blundering attempts to help you. You don't pretend anything. Your feelings show in you face . . . ' He watched Anna bite her lip.

'I'm not sure I like that. I'm supposed to be an actress, able to hide what I'm really feeling!'

'When you're on stage, you can, but you're so sensitive to everything, you change colour a dozen times a second, your eyes are always giving you away.' He took her hands and kissed the palms gently. 'Darling. I love your honesty and your vulnerability, don't ever change.'

'Don't, Laird,' she said in distress, and he looked puzzled. 'Don't begin by laying down conditions,' she stammered, trying to explain. 'I don't know if I will ever change, but if I do I won't be doing it deliberately—we all change, don't we? You can't make rules about it. You may change, too, but that won't mean I'll stop loving you.'

'I've changed a hell of a lot,' he said ruefully. 'Since I met you. You changed me the day I ran into you outside the theatre. That was a world-shaking collision, I haven't been the same since.' He smiled at her teasingly. 'I wanted you the minute I saw you.'

'I wanted you, too,' Anna said in a husky voice.

'Oh, good!' said Laird, his hand sliding, and she caught it between both her own, laughing at him.

'Stop that, I'm being serious! We still have a lot to work out. My career, for instance!'

'I wouldn't want to interfere with that!'

'I wouldn't let you,' she said simply, and he smiled.

'No, I didn't somehow think you would! It means a lot to you, doesn't it, darling?'

'Until recently, everything.'

His face softened at the way she looked at him. 'So it isn't always going to win against me? Well, I'm glad your career matters! I think Merieth might not have acted the way she did if she hadn't had such an empty life. She wouldn't have a baby in case it ruined her fun, she didn't want a job, so she filled in her life with mindless pleasure. Sex, drink, even drugs—it killed her in the end. It may even have been partly my fault—I gave her too much money, too much freedom. She abused both.'

'It's stupid to blame yourself. We're all responsible for what happens to us, but not for other people. They have to take the responsibility for their own lives. You didn't deliberately hurt Merieth, did you? No, whatever was wrong with her probably began before she even met you.' Anna looked dreamily at him. 'I want children, do you?'

He looked amused. 'Right away, you mean?'

'No, I have too much to cope with at the moment —acting and you, too. But one day!'

His eyes were dark with tenderness. 'Whenever you want to start the process, darling, I'm your man!'

She laughed. 'One-track mind!'

'You've had a pretty tough life, haven't you?' Laird asked her gently. 'No family, no security, no money . . . just the theatre and your dreams. Let me take care of you from now on—I keep offering and you keep turning me down, but this time you'll listen, won't you? You'll take the TV commercial job? It will be quite a nice sum of money, you won't have to worry until the West End run begins.'

She considered him, her eyes half-closed. 'What a very persistent wolf you are!'

'Little pig, little pig, let me in, let me in,' he wheedled, and with a husky little groan Anna put her arms around his neck and stopped arguing.

Coming in April
Harlequin Category Romance Specials!

Look for six new and exciting titles from this mix of two genres.

4 Regencies—lighthearted romances set in England's Regency period (1811-1820)

2 Gothics—romance plus suspense, drama and adventure

Regencies

Daughters Four by Dixie Lee McKeone
She set out to matchmake for her sister, but reckoned without the Earl of Beresford's devilish sense of humor.

Contrary Lovers by Clarice Peters
A secret marriage contract bound her to the most interfering man she'd ever met!

Miss Dalrymple's Virtue by Margaret Westhaven
She needed a wealthy patron—and set out to buy one with the only thing she had of value....

The Parson's Pleasure by Patricia Wynn
Fate was cruel, showing her the ideal man, then making it impossible for her to have him....

Gothics

Shadow over Bright Star by Irene M. Pascoe
Did he want her shares to the silver mine, her love—or her life?

Secret at Orient Point by Patricia Werner
They seemed destined for tragedy despite the attraction between them....

CAT88A-1

Harlequin Intrigue
Adopts a New Cover Story!

We are proud to present to you
the new Harlequin Intrigue cover design.

Look for two exciting new stories each month, which
mix a contemporary, sophisticated romance with the
surprising twists and turns of a puzzler . . . romance
with "something more."

ATTRACTIVE, SPACE SAVING BOOK RACK

Display your most prized novels on this handsome and sturdy book rack. The hand-rubbed walnut finish will blend into your library decor with quiet elegance, providing a practical organizer for your favorite hard-or soft-covered books.

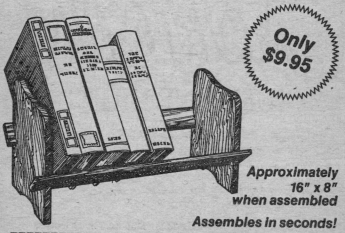

Only $9.95

Approximately 16" x 8" when assembled

Assembles in seconds!

To order, rush your name, address and zip code, along with a check or money order for $10.70* ($9.95 plus 75¢ postage and handling) payable to *Harlequin Reader Service*:

Harlequin Reader Service
Book Rack Offer
901 Fuhrmann Blvd.
P.O. Box 1396
Buffalo, NY 14269-1396

Offer not available in Canada.

BKR-1A

*New York and Iowa residents add appropriate sales tax.

HARLEQUIN SIGNATURE EDITION

CAROLE MORTIMER

JUST ONE NIGHT

Hawk Sinclair—Texas millionaire and owner of the exclusive Sinclair hotels, determined to protect his son's inheritance. Leonie Spencer—desperate to protect her sister's happiness.

They were together for just one night.
The night their daughter was conceived.

Blackmail, kidnapping and attempted murder add suspense to passion in this exciting bestseller.

The success story of Carole Mortimer continues with *Just One Night*, a captivating romance from the author of the bestselling novels, *Gypsy* and *Merlyn's Magic*.

**Available in March
wherever paperbacks are sold.**

WTCH-1